D1055631

DEAN B. ELLIS LIBRARY
ARKANSAS STATE UNIVERSITY

BLACKBIRD

BOOKS BY IVAN SOUTHALL FOR YOUNG PEOPLE

The *Simon Black* series
Hills End
Ash Road
The Fox Hole
To the Wild Sky
Let the Balloon Go
Finn's Folly
Chinaman's Reef Is Ours
Bread and Honey
Josh
Over the Top
Head in the Clouds
Matt and Jo
Seventeen Seconds
Three Novels (omnibus edition)
Fly West
What about Tomorrow
King of the Sticks
The Golden Goose
The Long Night Watch
A City Out of Sight
Christmas in the Tree
Rachel

B L A C K B I R D

Ivan Southall

Farrar Straus Giroux
New York

WITHDRAWN
From the
Dean B. Ellis Library
Arkansas State University

DEAN B. ELLIS LIBRARY
ARKANSAS STATE UNIVERSITY

To Dōnal Campbell Menzies

Copyright © 1988 by Ivan Southall
All rights reserved
Library of Congress catalog card number: 88-45328
Published simultaneously in Canada by Collins Publishers, Toronto
Printed in the United States of America
Designed by *Trish Parcell Watts*
First edition, 1988

Lib.Sci.
F
S&87bl
1988

Contents

518404

Sufficient to assert that
the characters of the loudmouth
and his kid
and of their falsely accused opponent
are not a fiction

1. A Perilously Unfortified Position

Hadden dominated the valley. It was the key to the defence of the Australian Alps. The key to all things visible and all things out of sight. The control point. The axis. The Great City. Every day it remained, undefended victory for the Allies was farther off. Yet not a weapon in sight to defend it. Not a defensive obstacle to delay an enemy assault.

Out there, in that snowbound land, lost under its black and awesome skies, trainee pilots not yet competent to survive combat were threatened whenever they left the ground. Out there Dad's enormous pro-

ject—whatever it might have been—was directly open
to air attack. Out there, though you couldn't see them,
the military roads heading north, over which passed
continuous convoys of troops and supplies, lay vul-
nerable and exposed.

"For unprincipled negligence," Will said, "it takes
the biscuit. What's wrong at Southern Command?"

He went on backing off, step by step, broadening
his view of the big house, now dipping his head, as if
shy, aware that his alarm was turning to fear. No.
Define that, please, as *severe professional appre-
hension.*

What would the result of this negligence be? Even
if well-planned defensive works were established at
once? In enemy attack, of course. Bitter, determined,
and repeated enemy attack. Even if on one day the
enemy formations were driven back, next day they'd
attack again, and victory for either side would never
be more than the breathing space of a few hours.

If Will fortified Hadden today, he'd be defending it
tomorrow and countless days thereafter. Against the
Japanese Second Army. An army of a hundred thousand men. Every man a master of disguise. The crack-
erjack army of a million faces.

So you might find Turks there—or the illusion of
Turks—thousands of them. Or the Tartar hordes of
Genghis Khan like a storm battering at the gates.

You'd never know in what century, with what
weapons, or in what disguise, you'd be required to
meet this infinitely ingenious foe.

"By George, Jackson, if we're awarding points, the General Staff of Southern Command scores none from me."

"Will!" A shout from the Colonel. "Watch your step! You'll be flat on your back on the next terrace down!"

Soldiers, rarely asked to face the challenge of moving heavy furniture, were stumbling up flights of stone steps from level to level of the neglected terraced gardens between the road and the house. They were confining their reasonable complaints to a form of breathless banter. Not so the Colonel's wife.

Something was getting at the fine lady. This the soldiers observed. Colonels had their troubles, it seemed. Perhaps colonels aimed high and got landed with complications that men in the ranks never had to worry about.

They were glancing, too, at Geoffrey and his lapel badge of the Aircrew Reserve. And at the athletic Patricia who might blossom into an interesting young lady. And at the kid. At Will. Years later the former Corporal Coulson was to say, "Like anyone's kid. Like one of my own. You'd never have guessed."

Dad's area of operations was out there in the invisible distances. Out there Colonel Phillip James Houghton was top man. Moving mountains or rivers that you'd not know about unless you'd keenly read the map.

"The cold's in my bones, Phillip," Mum said, not

letting up, an edge to her voice. "Surely you couldn't have imagined I wouldn't care?" She was embarrassing her children. "For once I understand the viewpoint of the miserable cat. He'd be happier if we'd thrown him to the crocodiles."

Oh, this neglected old house at the outskirts of this rundown one-street town under skies as black as the hat you'd wear in mourning for your lost life.

"You know what I'm like in the cold, Phillip. You know the best of me dies in it."

"Weather comes and goes," Dad said huskily. "You've got to live somewhere safe, Marjorie. It's the best I could do in the little time I have. I wanted you out of danger. I wanted you in reach."

A sigh, but a set to his jaw.

"As for you, Will," Dad went on, "your present occupation is not the reviewing of defences, but mucking in with the rest of us, moving anything you're strong enough to carry. I will not have my soldiers driving back into that country in the dark."

Well, each rosy-faced kid had his day. He played around for as long as he could; then they got him.

"Do you," Dad had asked in his letters, "propose to sit around up north waiting to have your heads cut off? Have you given invasion a thought? The only able-bodied man worth relying on being Geoffrey, and Geoffrey's about to leave you. What then? Will you be expecting Will to carry the responsibility? Expecting a boy to become a regiment of soldiers? If you fail

4

to leave voluntarily, you, and the rest of the settlement, will be ordered out.

"This might not be our view of a just world," Dad wrote, "but common sense compels you to come down here now before you're driven out or made the tragic casualties of war. I have acquired a property.

"The nature of our enemy must be clear to you. A resourceful foe who considers that quaint rules of combat attractive to us have nothing to do with his idea of war.

"In my nightmares I see you spiked by bayonets and pinned to your precious banana trees."

Unloading the trucks and reeling laden up flight after flight of steps to the house. Up and down. Back and forth across the terraces. Everyone "mucking in."

Once, on the highest terrace, just below verandah level, Dad waved into the east. "Out there," he said, "when the view opens up, it'll take your breath." Then he continued as if reading from a weather report, "But for now, those great primeval forests are groaning and rending beneath the weight of record early snows."

Mum said dryly, "I've made it clear in their lessons, Phillip, that the arduous measuring of records is a waste of money and time. They last but an hour and fade away. The Aboriginal had permanence. And brains. He accepted the course of Nature as it came and in the old times headed north from here before the seasons changed."

"Oh, do let's go to the snow, Dad," Will pleaded.

"Don't be hard on us. Why bother fighting for the blinkin' country if we can't even see the snow?"

"I'd reckon, Dad," Patricia said, "you really should spare yourself a thought. You'll be getting known round here as the mean old man who brought his kids down from the tropics and wouldn't take 'em to the snow."

Even Geoffrey was showing interest. An improvement upon his recent dispirited state. Geoffrey now standing by for the moment with the cat, with Anvil, sullen and bedraggled in his cage.

"No one goes anywhere," Mum said. "The Army doesn't rank round here and I'm not available for consultation until the house is habitable. With stacks of dry wood to window level and fires alight and everything thoroughly aired. We've got to sleep in this morgue tonight. It's colder in there than out-of-doors. Ridiculous. Even if you gain your father's consent, you won't get mine."

"There's no conflict, Marjorie," Dad said. "There really isn't, but I'd like everyone to remember that the Army's been extraordinarily good. They've shipped you from there to here without any haggle. But if I took you to the snow they'd string me up."

"They'd *never* string up the Colonel," shrilled Will.

"Colonels are answerable. Along with generals and admirals. And the pilots of aeroplanes. As Geoffrey will learn. Even the King's answerable."

"The King's not answerable!"

"I hope you don't believe that, Will. Watch Anvil, Geoffrey. Particularly later. Don't open that cage until he's calm and protect yourself while you're at it. I suggest you keep him in the house for a week before you show him the great outdoors or he'll be gone for good."

In an hour Dad himself had gone.

They'd come two thousand miles, hadn't seen him in months, and he hadn't even stopped for tea.

There they were, everything piled up around them, everything just arrived, everything looking as if they were about to leave, just as it had looked back home, so recently, two thousand miles away in the lovely warm.

Unbelievably, Dad touched his cap and went away, back to the construction site, wherever or whatever it might have been, taking the men and the vehicles with him.

Quickly out of sight and hearing.

Quickly gone.

2. Houghton Sorbet

Will thought it might be break of day at last. "Oh, please," he said, "the night's got to be gone. It's the longest night since I was born."

The bare window over there . . . The ragged blind that had crashed three-quarter way to the ceiling at 3 a.m., frightening the life half out of him, slapping round and round and round . . . The watery-looking rectangle of glass, for there were no curtains yet . . .

It really was day, day of a kind, Day Two at the big house called Hadden.

What a way to return to the world from the painless

realm of sleep where even the weather didn't hurt. Coming back, finding himself on a tiny island of lukewarmth, trying to climb into the pockets of his pajama top. The bottoms being unspeakable.

And taking note of the fact that this was but the dawning of Day Two, which meant the rest of his days were lying in wait like the siege of the Great City—set about by endless ranks of enemy soldiers armed with icicles shaped like spears and swords and knives.

Sleep a thousand nights. Die a thousand deaths.

Next the happy fellows, dressed in black with black silk hats and anticipatory smiles, would be sidling through the door to fold Will's arms and close his eyes and address him in tones like the insides of big bass drums:

"Corpses do *not* peep over the top of the sheet! Most improper, kid, when time is at hand for going to ground. There to enjoy the clever economies devised by us patriots to hasten an Allied victory. Like not bothering with flowers stinking up the place. All the flowers going to the soldiers, sailors, and airmen to wear in their buttonholes, to pretty up the battle-fields. And, provided by us, a most handsome coffin without a bottom or top. The timbers thus saved going to the soldiers, sailors, and airmen to whittle in their spare time into the shape of gigantic guns, thus de-ceiving the enemy and bringing glorious victory due to our cleverness. Yet we're asking nothing in return except a small advance to cover the hardships we're suffering and to meet the cost of the widows and orphans tax."

"Very generous I'm sure," Will thought. "Yet when I get into this deathtrap again, I'll be wearin' all my clothes, including my boots, though it strikes me I'm hearing a heavy silence out where my breakfast should be gettin' ready. I don't hear anyone lightin' that fire. I don't hear anythin' except Old Pop Houghton squeaking like a nest of mice."

Which reminded Will of Anvil, the pussycat. And that any food on hand would be fed to *him*. Mum already having expressed her feelings upon the matter. Mum last evening, exhausted, but trying to be her usual droll self, suffering remorse perhaps for having embarrassed everybody, for having behaved so badly.

"Pussycats have to be fed right," she'd said. "Pussycats don't understand the ways of the world. Any more than I understand the ways of the pussycat. But it's not the wretched animal's fault he's been boxed up for a week. Nor mine either. It's not his fault he's as mad as a tiger snake. I'm as mad as one, too. Pussycats are helpless, innocent creatures. Like me. Pussycats don't start wars. I don't either, except by accident, and then I never know what to do with them. *Don't pat him! He'll bite your hand off!*"

"I'll bet," Will said, addressing the blanket over his head, "that some miserable beggar's crept up on me during the night, stuck a stamp on me, and posted me to the South Pole. I'll bet you all those beggars out there have had their breakfasts and ducked out to lunch at the pub.

"I'll bet you there's nothing left to eat out there except the scrapings in the bin, but I'm ordering two eggs fried on both sides and two crisp rashers of bacon with *lots* of hot-buttered toast. I'd put it in writing, except I'd get a lecture about there being a war on. About humans being different from pussycats. About the pilots having to eat the eggs and bacon because they don't know whether they're going to come back or not. The poor pilots having the right to a last meal of my lovely eggs and bacon. That bein' my contribution to the war effort. So I hope they eat up good and hearty or it's a terrible waste."

Will tightening more into his little ball on his tiny island. Each slash of the freezing cold surrounding him slicing off another strip of Houghton Sorbet. Notably at the back where the bottom of his jacket didn't meet the top of his pants. *Sorbet à la derrière à la Houghton.*

Nothing living outside raising even a twitter. Nothing with fur on or feathers on or even a little pair of woolly mitts. Which meant the birds would be hanging upside down on their little frozen twigs by their little frozen toes. Might be excuses for the Houghtons just arrived from the tropics, but the stupid birds got *born* here.

So Will said, "I have an announcement. I'm getting

out of this rotten bed and never getting back in. I'm making myself some breakfast and then I'm goin' home. Anyone surviving a night round here can walk two thousand miles like falling off a roof. If the Japs get there before me, too bad. I'll live down a hole or up a tree."

He thrust his bare feet to the floor where the cold linoleum struck him almost breathless, and a mist was on the windowpane as if it had been raining a drizzle inside the room.

Yesterday Mum had said the weather was ridiculous.

Will reached out for a touch of the icy glass and slowly shook his head. "People don't live here because they want to. They get sent here instead of going to gaol."

His touch made a peephole in the mist. So he peered through and grumbled. "I don't know how a fellow's supposed to believe it."

Outside, the mist was like a wall that might have gone on to fill the world. Everything had melted into it but for a few tree trunks looking like left-overs from ancient Rome. No other identifiable form of life or habitation—except one small bird.

"Well, bless your little cotton socks," Will said.

A bird of enormous industry, fat, black, and sleek, yellow rimmed eyes and a bright orange beak, scratching in an overgrown flower bed against the verandah.

"Sink me," Will said. "The last creature left on

Earth. How do you stand it, mate? Why don't you fly away to the warm?"

His frowning face at the windowpane failed to excite the bird, as his reasonable suggestion that it should seek a warmer clime failed to interest it.

"You're not very bright," Will said.

But the bird went on scratching, first with one leg, then the other, flicking its head, dispatching with beak and claw fragments of dead leaves and twigs and lumps of dirt in numerous directions.

"You're a criminal type, I fear," Will said, "of the genus *blackbird,* I'd reckon. I've heard about your kind. Stuffed to the gills with friends and neighbours. The criteria being that your friends should taste good. Can you imagine me eating Anvil?"

These comments the busy bird regarded as unworthy of attention.

Will said, "You're giving your species a bad name, mate, seeing you're the first blackbird I've met. You should be trying to create a good impression. All these humans writing poetry about blackbirds for hundreds of years. You ought to be ashamed. Tearing the countryside to bits. D'you fancy being remembered like Attila the Hun?"

Will then felt moved to add, "You'll get a pain mixing soup and main course and dessert. You should keep 'em separate, mate. Reckless gluttony's a dangerous habit. Didn't your mother tell you it was the skinny birds who died of old age? You'll end up in a pie. You'll get set before the king and he'll wash you down with a flagon of ale and he won't even care."

The blackbird didn't care either.

"I'm wastin' my time on you," Will said.

Shortly, out in the lofty hall, after a notably chilly experience in the bathroom:

"Shiver me," Will said to Old Pop Houghton, "that was a real reckless exercise. What do you reckon my chances are of holding off till summer?"

Pop, leaning against the wall about half-way to the kitchen, expressed in reply the opinion that it was 7:53, though there wouldn't be another clock in the house to agree with him. Pop's estimate serving to remind Will that the Houghtons were still only sixteen hours off the train.

"I think that's just terrible," Will said. "Considering me being frozen half to death. Up at home by this hour I'd be frolicking in the sun, collecting the coconuts washed in on the tide. So it's a gobble of breakfast, then back to Capricornia."

In the kitchen Mum was sitting at the table.

What was *she* doing out of bed?

Sprawled all over the place, most unlike her, wrapped in a fair proportion of the less fashionable garments she owned, massing to twice her usual size, more like someone Will mightn't have met before, grey with cold, black shadows in the lines of her face, an empty coffee jug and a ruinous heap of cigarette butts at her elbow.

First time he knew she smoked!

Maybe she'd just started and pinched them from Geoffrey.

Imagine meeting someone strange all dressed up in the contents of your mother's wardrobe!

"Sit down," she said.

Her voice was slurred. Talk about stumbling onto the secret life. Maybe she had a private hoard of hooch. Maybe she went flying across the rooftops on a broomstick when Old Pop Houghton struck midnight!

"Make yourself at home, my son, seeing we're stuck with each other. Pull up a chair. Help yourself to disgusting limp cracker biscuits. Help yourself to anything that takes your fancy. Everything's uniformly lousy."

"Please, Mum, no."

"Please no what?"

"Please may I go back to my nice warm bed, Mum."

"Sit down, my son."

She was dull-eyed and puffy-lipped and he'd never heard her make use of the term *my son*. He didn't go for it.

"Sit down when you're told," she said, "and choose your poison. Dregs of black coffee. Dregs of black tea. Nothing hot until someone lights the fire. Nothing fresh until the shops open. If the fog ever lifts. If there's anything out there other than a great hole with the world at the bottom of it."

What was he to say?

"I thought you were Geoffrey Stevenson Houghton," she said. "Aircrew Reserve. Tripping quietly by. But not so. And how charming if you'd been your handsome father. Like the return of the age of miracles. With menfolk, my son, I have the Midas touch. All encounters turn to gold. With the literal exception of you."

Will looked into his lap.

"And even you have reached the age of ultimate wisdom. Time to know your mother's flawed. Time to wake up and know it all. If you don't know it by now, it can't be worth knowing, can it?"

There wasn't anything he was brave enough to utter.

"How'd you sleep, my son, in this gala first night spent within the halls of our stately home?"

He swallowed hard to make a voice. "It wasn't all that marvellous. I was cold."

"And the jolly old same goes for jolly old me," she said and poked an exploratory finger into the empty cigarette pack. "You have plans for today, my son?"

"Plans?"

"With a *p* and an *l* and an *a* and an *n* and an *s*. Everyone has plans. Expectations. Hopes."

His anxiety showed. "There must be lots to see. I suppose . . . I suppose I could take a walk . . ."

"Meaning in the direction of a former coral strand?"

He couldn't believe it. It had never been more than a half-baked idea.

"No, Mum . . . Who'd do a stupid thing like that?"

"Check your sums, my son. Two thousand miles is two thousand miles. Did you know much of it is a wilderness? Did you know you'd die on the way? Did you know your crow-pecked remains might never be found?"

He began to feel a tightening inside. "Yeh, Mum."

"Two thousand miles is an unreasonable expectation even for a young lion. Even before the rot of the years reduces you to the level of me."

"Yeh, Mum."

"So we have areas of agreement. That's nice. Areas of disagreement also press upon us."

He was getting alarmed for her.

"I've been wanting a talk with you, Will. Long overdue. About little-boy games. Like playing soldiers. They become inappropriate. They frazzle my nerves. No one's expecting you to assume the wisdom of King Solomon overnight, but if you're thinking of beginning the great trek, why not try setting course for the outskirts of civilized behaviour?"

"I don't know what you mean, Mum."

"Oh yes you do, Will Houghton. Here we are among the blizzards. Neither of us totally stuffed to the ears with stupidity. Except that we've allowed ourselves to be bullied into making this absurd move. Couldn't be a better place to lay the ghosts or outgrow idle play. Life's basic down here, my son. It's survive or perish."

"I don't know what you mean."

"Of course you do, Will Houghton."

There was more of it and it got worse. Mum was in a mood. Day Two at the house called Hadden looked like carrying on from where Day One had left off.

Will's heartbeat quickened and the adrenaline sharpened his wits. It needed to.

3. Haworth Revisited

No word came from Dad for three days and Mum seemed to lose the will to pull herself together, huddling beside one fire or another, poking at the flames, sighing like an old grandmother, drinking strong tea, shaking her head.

They'd not seen her demoralised before.

"The other face of love," she said, not for their hearing, though they heard it just the same.

Outside, the fog remained, as if it were the nature of the land.

Dad at last appeared at the door, tense from a long

and dangerous run through the mountains, in the company of his driver, who waited in the entry, and of his adjutant, who came on in.

They were passing through, Dad said.

Well, they were heading for Command, and coming by this road in present conditions was not necessarily longer than by any other. They'd appreciate a quick lunch and a nice pot of tea all round.

Afterwards, Mum was beside herself.

"Out of the *goodness* of his heart he comes by *this* road because it's not longer than *other* roads! In he comes with half the regiment. With chaperones. I don't want to see his adjutant. I don't want to see his driver. Am I the cookhouse skivvy? Is he Commanding Officer or isn't he?"

"He did right, Mum," Geoffrey said gently.

"Right for what?"

"For his first responsibility."

"His first *what*?"

"For good order and discipline, Mum. First and foremost he's the Colonel. He must do things right and be seen to be doing them right."

"Does my firstborn presume to lecture me on first principles? That principles are all I may have of his father? Why should his principles outrank mine? I've lived at the bottom of the list, my lad, since you were knee-high to a bicycle. Now, with your blessing, he puts the holy seal of war upon it. I might as well have married a ghost. Now you see him. Now you don't.

The foundation stones of half the defence establishments of the South Pacific bear his name. Yet he pursued me round the world to make me his wife. What of then and what of now?"

He returned in another four days and stayed an hour and a quarter for tea and hot scones.

After he'd gone, Mum sat grey and still and wept silently from rage.

At the evening table she said, "He's obsessed with conscience, with propriety, with self-sacrifice. When we were thousands of miles apart I could live with it because I knew there was no alternative. He should have left us as we were. Realistically, what danger was there? Would they have bothered to invade? Will they ever? Why invade fourteen private houses and three pineapple farms?"

"It depends, Mum," Will said, "upon the broader strategy, and we haven't any idea of what that might be."

She turned a baleful eye on him. "How old is this pompous young bore?"

(Will thought: You're gettin' insultin', Mum. People are listenin'.)

"*Hadden,*" she said. "Is that what they call it? *Haworth* would have been more to the point. The Parsonage revisited. You watch us start dying of consumption."

"There's a war on, Mum," Geoffrey felt compelled to say.

She turned on him with anger. "Yes; and I don't need you to remind me of it."

He flushed and left the room and allowed his meal to go to waste. And went without breakfast for two days. And lunched frugally and moodily at the pub, arousing some curiosity, until his allowance ran out.

Family connections of the Houghtons live to this day on the broad acres where the big house was.

After the great fires of 1962, only stalks, stumps, chimneys, and grotesque ruins like the devastation of a battle were left in a wasteland, a charred and rocky hollow marking the site of the Geoffrey Houghton Lily Pond—laboriously constructed in 1944 by Mum's own hand and spanned by a small Japanese tea-garden bridge.

4. Honour of the Regiment

Now to the first fine day. And to the roof and the ascent of it. Followed by the ridge. And by what was to become of the honour of the regiment.

The fine day. Day Ten. After which the count lapsed and days began to merge.

Seven forty-five in the morning and there it was.

A glare on the bedroom blind such as Will hadn't seen since they'd left the lovely Tropic of Capricorn. Since they'd emptied the high and airy house and bolted the shutters and locked the doors and surrendered the keys to the property agent and gone away with him behind the Army vehicles; Mum sighing, looking like she could start crying; Geoffrey slumping in misery in the early stages of a broken heart; even Patricia giving a strident sniff.

The helpful property agent, using up rather too much of his monthly petrol ration to drive them to the train, might have spent the day more wisely conserving his fuel and exorcising the beach frontage of the despair they left behind. The spread of the infection would have prostrated any future client but the most foolhardy.

Will pulled up his bedroom blind—well, touched its edge—and it sprang wildly towards the ceiling.

Outside, coming through St. Sebastian's Gap, he met the blinding morning sun blazing across seas of frozen mist and sands of bitter frost.

Took his breath away.

Saturday, too.

"By George, Jackson, you'd better look here. No strain copping an eyeful of this."

It's there. It's what Dad said. When he comes in today we'll spike him to the wall like it was a banana tree and we were the Japs and he was us.

"Take us to the snow or else!"

Dad didn't come, so that fixed that.

Patricia came striding in, as if in pursuit of wild horses to break before breakfast.

"If you want your eyes pushed out through the back of your skull, boofhead, you should try clapping them on it from my room."

Geoffrey called from his Private Retreat (transplanted almost intact from Capricornia) of austerely framed watercolours painted by himself, of gilt-edged books written by scholars and poets, and volume upon volume of law, of his classical record collection and well-aged gramophone, of his modest selection of American cigars and cigarettes, and of photographs of Melanie aged thirteen, aged fourteen, and recently sixteen, Melanie demurely dressed as if for church, and in dresses like breezes, Melanie in a nineteenth-century gown, Melanie in sweaters and swimming costumes, and one in nothing at all, aged six months, an acquisition of which no member of her immediate family had been informed.

The guest entered Geoffrey's Private Retreat by invitation, upon which event one respectfully stood until offered a chair or a spot on the bed. Well, as Aircrew Reserve, he'd soon be a god in the sky. Like Kane. Like Finucane. Like Truscott.

"You two," Geoffrey called, "come on in here. The view from my window is worth the flight."

At breakfast Mum said, "It's not bad, you've got to admit."

But at lunch she was compelled to qualify. "It's colder than snow. It's the coldest sunshine . . . And we're here, mark my word, for the duration of a war that'll last a century . . . If he doesn't come home today, the rat . . ."

Geoffrey, aching for Melanie, believed himself to be close to the heart of what ailed Mum.

"It'll be all right in the end, Mum."

"I doubt it."

"It's got to be, Mum."

That they were conversing cordially was the best news in days. Marvellous what a bit of sunlight could do.

"The cold destroys me," she said. "Settles inside like a barium meal. That's something you wouldn't want to know about, that comes, my dears, from riotous living . . ."

The roof.

"She'll hear," Patricia hissed, "you clumsy great goof. Try thinking you're a mouse instead of a moose."

"It's all right for you," Will hissed back. "You with two flat feet flat on the ground. It's steep up here. Like the Matterhorn."

"Like the matter with what?"

"You know what I said, Patricia. You're trying to make me mad. You're trying to make me fall off."

"Keep your voice down, boofhead."

"It's slippery. It's got moss on it. There's ice in the cracks. We've got *glaciers* in the spouting. If you make me fall I'll get killed. Then I'll haunt you."

"You're yellow. Always your basic problem. A streak down your back as wide as your big boof head. You'd better let me go first."

"It's rusty old iron up here. It's got grey paint to make it look good. It's got nails stickin' up. You stay where you're safe. You'd break somethin', anyway. You're so fat you'd fall through and get stuck in the toilet."

"I'm not fat, you crude and horrible thing!"

"You're fat like a cow."

"I'm not meant to be like you. With bones sticking out all over. And I said keep your voice down!"

"Fat girl. Fat like a cow."

"I'll get you, boofhead!"

"What's going on out there?" Mum called.

"Nothing."

"I'd like to hear Will's opinion. Does he say it's nothing? Why doesn't he answer?"

"Because he's run off. The creep. The yellow-belly. He's teasing me. When he comes back I'll flatten him."

"There'll be no flattening, Patricia. I'll have you inside, thank you, where you can start behaving like a lady. There are matters to discuss that are long overdue. If we're forced to live among the blizzards, we're forced to face the chills of reality."

"No, Mum . . ."

"Why is it that my children when faced with the solids of life seek refuge behind the cry of *No, Mum*? As if it were a magic formula. As if it might put me to sleep for a hundred years. To begin with, in your brother's company, you're a hooligan. Bring a cukkle of scoke—a cukkle of . . . You know what I mean. Bring it."

"I don't bring in scuttles of coke. I'm a woman!"

"You're the one I've asked. And when you're a woman I'll tell you. Be quick through the door. We don't want the coke to get out. He'll be gone in a flash."

The beautiful day was flushed away. They had the ruin of the world and Mum with her spoonerisms.

Patricia hissed up the wall, "You creep. You flea. You and your loud mouth. You know what she means. It's the end that she means. When she gets the spooners it's always the end. She's going to peel me off like a bit of skin. It's going to be the former Patricia. I'm going to be the memory round here. I'll tell her you're up there."

"You'd *better* not!"

"I'll get you real good, boofhead. I'll get you good before I go. You'll curse the day you were born."

The ascent.

Will reckoned the best-looking spot on the ridge was the big double chimney where the house made an angle. There Mum would never see him from any reasonable position she might head for out-of-doors. This would have him passing the skinny chimney over Geoffrey's room from which issued the warbles of some lady opera singer.

Nerves of steel, Geoffrey had.

Like scaling a precipice, the face of that roof. Picks, you needed. Boots with spikes. And rope ladders dropping from the fellows who should have been going on in front. And no one was around to be impressed. All Will had was an icy cliff, with everywhere to miss a footing and nowhere soft to fall.

The crunch of his return to where the rocks and weeds and roses grew had a bit of tomorrow's certainty about it.

Grit the teeth and crawl then, clinging on with everything. It's the honour of the regiment, nothing else being left to fight for, with the hazards of the main living room and Mum's boudoir passing directly underneath.

So out came Patricia, as if he hadn't known, a slamming of the door, and a big rude grin.

She yelled, "You're dead right, Mum. I thought the dodo was extinct. Some clumsy-looking bird with hoofs like a horse and a tail like Will."

"Heave a brick at it, then!"

"As good as done, Mum."

It'd better bally well not be!

The stone she found was as big as an emu egg, and the harder he scrambled for the protection of the big chimney, the more he knew he'd never make it.

Tennis player that she was, with a serve like a cannonball and an eye like a gunsight, and the shock of the crash on the roof, significantly wide of the mark, signalled to Will that she wasn't really off her game.

From Geoffrey's skinny chimney there issued a shriek not on the opera score. "What the hell's going on?"

"Feathers sky high," Patricia yelled. "Frightened six months out of the brute."

"Stupid girl," shrilled Mum. "Frightened six months out of me!"

"Only doing what you said, Mum."

"You *knew* you weren't to take me literally! Your brains are in your biceps. Bring your useless brother in!"

"No sign of him, Mum."

The back door slammed again.

"Will."

Jumping Judas. It was Mum.

"Will!"

"He's gone off. I told you."

"I *wish* your father would come!"

"Yeh, Mum. I'll look for Will."

"You won't!"

"I'll find him, Mum. No trouble."

"You'll go immediately in. Watch out for the cat!"

The door slammed. Patricia was a good mate. Even if she was a girl and fifteen and fat.

The ridge.

Oh, the view that opened up!

Not an enemy this side of Kingdom Come would dare scratch his back or blink an eye or march the first step.

Hundreds of square miles out there under direct observation. Simply to observe was to freeze enemy movement, was to hold the Great City, was to win the battle. What a strategy. Conceived in a flash.

Brilliant mountains and forests of snow.

Brilliance as under a microscope directly lit.

The world as a bird might see it. Allowing for what the eye of a bird might be. Looking out over treetops, over the hotel and the post-office store, and the houses vainly trying to conceal themselves in copses, and then on and on into remote and glaring distances. As one would see from a low-flying, fast-flying aeroplane. If ever he was in such a thing in the way that Geoffrey would be.

An image of a little aeroplane like a swallow in Will's mind. "Go away from me," he said.

Little aeroplane like a swallow flashing over the treetops. Little aeroplane like an eagle flashing past the clifftops. Little aeroplane like a firestone striking the mountaintop.

"No," Will cried and his heart and eyes rushed back from the distance.

Suddenly very short on breath astride that rooftop and aware of the dizzying height of it.

Another image. The eagle. Poor young eagle born without a head for heights! Gliding in circles near the clifftop, stunned with fright, big fat sister flapping round yelling advice. The earth a sickening distance and almost out of sight.

No more images. Please.

How was he to get down when Mum called at three for afternoon tea with scones buttered hot from the oven?

How was he to get there with hands steady enough to hold the scones and lift the cup?

Soon he was unable to look up and was shorter yet on breath and feared he might choke in the layers of smoke from the living-room fire, eyes smarting, everywhere smoke, smoke from the big chimney, rising, bending, undulating, drooping to the sound of violins from Geoffrey's skinny chimney, smoke laced with nasty stuff from the kitchen flue and generated from the scuttle of coke.

Oh, for a breeze to take it up, but the wind was as still as a frozen breath.

Will feeling sick there, unable to raise his eyes to the view. Because he knew. The moment he looked, his senses would swim and he'd go tumbling and crashing and wailing and smashing to lie among the rocks and the weeds.

It might have been different with Patricia there. Something to work for with Patricia there. But nothing now to drive him on except the regimental honour, which fell kind of flat when you were all the officers and all the NCOs and all the men yourself.

Yet, if you were everyone in the regiment, didn't you carry all the honour upon yourself?

The sound of an aircraft engine fell upon him as if emptied from a vat. An instant later he heard the front door open and slam shut.

Heard Geoffrey yelling like someone very young, like someone small, like someone in a boyish flurry:

"Mum. Quick. Come and look, Mum. It's the first we've seen. A Wirraway from the flying school, Mum. Isn't she just beautiful? Quick, Mum. Oh, quick. She'll be gone in a flash."

Will clawed his fingers into the corrugations of the roof and bruised his legs into the ridge and looked.

Little aeroplane with the learner's yellow sash. Too low over the rooftops of Haddenham and a shattering blast from the engine as he took her away and up.

"She's gone, Mum. You were too slow."

"Too slow for what?"

"The Wirraway, Mum."

"I heard and saw," she said, "and don't ever you fly like that. The young man's a fool who'll not come back."

Will, on the rooftop, breath catching from smoke, trying to look out into the wide world over which the aeroplane vanished, everything spread out like a relief map in the general's tent, ready to receive the pins bearing standard abbreviations for Enemy Observation Post, Enemy Machine-Gun Position, Enemy Front Line, and others of the ilk. The kind of map requiring the kind of pins defined in *Open Warfare*, by Jackson, Volume 1, Appendix A.

The Wirraway observed no longer. A memory. As Patricia was about to be. And not a detail left upon the scene of Jackson's map. Only an idea that a map could have been.

"I know I can't get down," Will said, closing his eyes because the giddiness wouldn't go.

The days of little-boy games were to be left behind, Mum said, were to be left in the north where breezes were balmy on the sand. Where dreams were a reasonable and seasonable proposition all year round.

"Down here," Mum said, "where the blizzards blow, I'm asking you, my son, to journey along with the rest of us to the outer fringes of civilization."

Or something of the kind she'd said.

Sitting there in the kitchen those nine days ago.

"How about waking up one morning, my son, very soon, with a resolve to start seeing life for what life might be about. How about trying to live in the world we encounter, instead of the world that you imagine."

Something like that.

"Yeh, Mum," Will said. But at the time went on thinking: I don't go for talk like this. What's she getting at? These bits that might be another language?

"You're getting lanky, Will Houghton," she said. "Shooting up. Growing out of your boots. Growing out of your pants."

He didn't go for that either.

She said, "You'll be a tall man, my son. Might be striking. In a modest way. Aged forty-five. Greying at the temples. Had you noticed the changes coming on?"

"Not yet, Mum. Haven't noticed grey hairs yet, Mum."

She was a witch stirring up anxieties and dipping her spoon into the cauldron.

"It's no kind of world, Will, for the son of a family of high expectations, to go on living in fantasy land. Forever playing little-boy games. Stupid war games."

A groan inside Will.

"Your brother," she said, "is committed to war as it's fought between men. It happens to be his destiny. It happens to be the fate of most young men in these sorrowful days. The price they pay for having been born. Do you hear me, Will Houghton?"

"Yeh, Mum."

"But your generation, my son, will be asked to rebuild the world. That's what you'll be asked to pay for having come along four or five years later. That's all that it takes. For some the stain and pain of war. For others the virtue of reconstruction. Nothing lying between but a few lousy years."

"Yeh, Mum."

"I'm of the opinion, my son, that you two brothers were born the wrong way about. Have you suspected that you're the destroyer and he's the builder?"

"Yeh, Mum."

The words went round and round in his giddiness on the ridge.

"This is chance, my son. Chance becoming destiny. Destiny becoming fate. Fate becoming the direction one's generation takes. That's what each of us is asked to give. The life that fulfils the direction of one's own generation whether one's temperament is suited to it or not."

"Yeh, Mum."

"If I hear that primitive response one more time I'll hit you with a saucepan."

"Yeh, Mum."

"Oh, my *God*!"

For the first time, he saw it clear and knew it plain and respected her point of view, though the way she put it didn't amuse him and he kept a wary eye on the saucepans.

She started drumming her fingertips on the table and looking like Anvil out of sorts. She took a long, whistling breath through her elegant teeth.

"You weren't born in a year, Will Houghton, that was fated to go on tearing the world down, but that's the dream you live with. How much more am I supposed to stand? A gentle son fated to ravage the Earth. The other little horror obsessed with war games."

"That's me, Mum."

"I'll do you in, Will, if you keep this up."

There was, surprisingly, a hardening of his heart without any hostility and a hardening of his voice that brought bright lights to her tired eyes.

"No you won't, Mum."

After a time she said, "You're not to play dumb with me ever again. I detect a few results from the nails of truth I've been hammering into you."

"Whatever you say, Mum."

She might have been a short distance ahead.

"I've had a wretched night," she then said, those nine days ago, and flicked the cigarette pack across the table at his chest.

"Yeh, Mum. So have I."

"Take a cue from your father, my son. He dreams of rivers tamed, of tunnels under mountains, of bridges built. An unusual soldier. But he drives me almost to drink for reasons that one day, even to you, may make sense. I honour him. He walks a straight path. His dreams I like. I wish to honour you also. Have you a label yet for your dreams?"

"Yeh, Mum."

"Then let me hear of your dreams."

Jackson could have put it concisely.

Will's eyes narrowed and saw instead of his mother the printed page, an uncommon page, for Jackson rarely wrote upon such matters. Extraordinary. For then he was able to convert Jackson's page to the spoken word:

"Madam. The world we have is our inheritance. It's not of our own making. I see no sign that your son is unaware of it. To the contrary, you cannot predict he'll not need to defend his sister or, by some twist of fate, his father or his brother. Or himself. Or you. If you would have him survive to practise the arts of peace, assist him to acquire the arts of war. Countless years, madam, show that the strength of the strong is the shield of the weak. But the weak and the untrained and the fools would have themselves and everyone else dead for the sake of their own failure to take account of the greed of less principled men. The strong and thoroughly trained are soon enough honourably dead as it is."

The silence was stunned.

She held to a handful of hair.

"I've spawned a monster."

"Will!"

It was Mum. Not nine days ago at the kitchen table, but here. And now.

"Are you there, Will?"

Yeh, Mum . . . Stuck up on the roof like someone you wouldn't want to know . . .

"You're to come. Or I'll give your scones to the cat. I've had enough of this nonsense."

I've had enough of it, too, Mum. But there's nothing I can do. I've made a terrible mistake, Mum. Like you and your menfolk, everything I touch turns to gold.

I can't answer and I can't come.

And I really am sorry, Mum.

5. Blind Corner

Time changed for later and cold changed for colder. The weakening of the light was the worst.

Mum's voice, heard at the fringes, changed also.

"I require you to stop these absurd and inappropriate games. You're not accustomed to this degree of cold."

Patricia's voice changed, too. "Don't let the team down, Will. Come on, wherever you are. Stop fooling around!"

Everything in Will's head and heart changed and the funny things about being alive failed to raise a smile inside as before. Often doing a moan on the outside for the entertainment of one and all, but not on the inside where he lived with himself.

Jackson had a good way of putting it: General George Jackson with his string of decorations deriving more from diplomacy than from war. "Keep them guessing, soldier. While they're guessing, the game's in your court."

"Will! For pity's sake, come indoors!"

A bit of tomfoolery turned a blind corner and nothing was waiting when you got there.

An emptiness was lying ahead, and an emptiness lay behind. All he had left was the corner in the middle. Nowhere to stay and no way of going back or going on. As if the ridge had become a small rock with great seas all around.

"It's half past four and you'll catch your death out there."

You don't hear me arguing, Mum.

Soon, they'd know he was scared.

Well, worse than scared.

Then every time they saw him, or a thought of him crossed their minds, they'd remember Will frozen with cowardice. Afraid of answering. Afraid of helping himself. Almost afraid of breathing the air.

Will hadn't turned out to be the fellow they'd supposed.

He didn't know how he'd live with the shame, or how he'd face Dad, or front up to Geoffrey eye to eye.

"Will!"

Nothing ever again would be the same.

Or he'd really catch his death of cold. Real death of real cold. And not feel anything anymore.

When the light went, when the dark came, he'd freeze on the ridge.

His body would go numb like poor Scott and his companions on the way home from the Pole.

So he'd fall, but not to glide in circles like a young eagle in a funk, tipped by the big fat sister from the family eyrie into empty heights.

The fall would be the end of it.

6. Law Degree Deferred

Geoffrey Stevenson Houghton. Named for the maternal grandfather, a passionate, scholarly, and idealistic man, now dead.

Geoffrey, aged nineteen years three months and a day or two.

Of this branch and generation of the Houghton family, the firstborn. Traditionally, the heir. But, in realistic terms, the Houghton least likely to live long enough to inherit or to fulfil any objectives other than short-term.

His long-term objectives, a dream, were in law.

Taking first things first. The planting of the seed: acquiring the background, the knowledge, the degree.

The growth to follow: the amassing of experience, law for all the people, law for those who could pay, law for those who couldn't pay, law to correct the wrong, good law confirmed and made strong, bad law repealed and rewritten at its source.

Geoffrey Stevenson Houghton, Member of Parliament. Tireless and incorruptible servant. Leader of men.

His law degree deferred at the end of first year. To be resumed if peace returned, and the right side won, and Geoffrey came home with life, limb, nervous system, and mental faculties reasonably intact.

Meanwhile, he went on living through a long season of limbo, self-consciously wearing the lapel pin that informed interested persons he was about to become a fledgling.

Perhaps when the trainee fighter pilots from the flying school arrived in town by road once a month, Geoffrey might take his place beside them in the afternoon to enjoy the modest hospitality at the pub. Wearing his lapel pin proudly; for others might then take note of it and begin to care, for few in this remote place understood what it was.

Geoffrey waiting for no one knew what. Waiting with calm or anxiety or fear? No one knew that either, except Geoffrey, and no one expected him to discuss his state of mind.

Geoffrey waiting with a strange, intense, and perplexed longing to face the ultimate music, to be a pilot, to get it over, to live or die and achieve. To achieve anything.

To be any kind of pilot.

Of single-engine fighters or twin-engine fighters or multi-engine bombers or, less likely, of flying boats or stork-like machines equipped for special duties or reconnaissance. Anything, as long as the control column in his hands directed the purpose and the majesty of flight.

Or, otherwise, in a disappointment he dreaded, he'd be transferred to another branch of the human race.

He'd be an observer.

Or an air gunner.

Or a flight engineer.

Or a wireless operator.

Or an airborne specialist in some unpublicised department of practical science, presiding over miraculous secret equipment, the precise nature of which he would not utter aloud, for the enemy's ears were all around; behind the mirror, under the bed, concealed in every bus and train and café and hotel bar. Even in the smile of the lovely lady.

The Air Force could not be more precise about the future, until Geoffrey demonstrated that he was fitted best for one activity or another. Or demonstrated that he was fit for nothing by failing to meet the demanding standards of physical health and mental competence.

That would be unthinkable.

Geoffrey studying each day in his Private Retreat from texts supplied by the Air Force, followed by repeated repetition in the presence of an available family member sworn to secrecy, if secrecy were required; usually Will, the eager beaver. Geoffrey learning by the ancient formula of rote. By drumming it in. By turning knowledge into an automatic response requiring no effort of recall. This, he was given to understand, might become the first and the last line between life and death.

The subjects:

Law and Administration, for the effectiveness of an officer or an NCO in his dealings with other ranks depended upon his confident action, without fear, favour or prejudice, in any reasonable situation he might be likely to encounter.

And *Theory of Flight,* for getting into the air in an aeroplane, effectively, and proceeding with the mission, efficiently, and getting down again with one's crew alive, depended upon specific knowledge and finesse in the application of the knowledge.

And *Engine Theory,* because surprise of surprises, blue-blooded engines of dazzling performance and stunning reputation were not built like bullock carts. They would buck at heavy-handed, heavy-footed misuse or childish showing-off. They demanded sensitive understanding and constant maintenance, or the life of the engine and of its human abuser were both at risk.

And *Aircraft Navigation and Meteorology,* because

the safety of his aeroplane, his crew, and of himself, would rest upon his ability to fly both ways, there and back, no matter what hazards the enemy or the weather might inflict upon him.

And *Aircraft Recognition,* because the hopes of everyone who relied upon him, or loved him, would depend upon his knowing instantly which machine was of enemy origin and which was not. The likely outcome of error or indecision was death.

And *Armaments,* because in the end everything would be in the safekeeping of armaments, or at the immediate disposal of armaments, whether they were the teeth of his own aeroplane or teeth used against him in combat. Armaments, either way, were sudden death.

Geoffrey studying each day, each day committing a little more to lifelong memory, yet each day despairing because Melanie was somewhere else.

Melanie was left where the coconuts came in on the tide, and where, according to Colonel Houghton, the Japanese might at any time appear.

In that other world far away, back there.

That other life in which he'd been a different young man of much lighter heart.

As if all that he had brought of Melanie to this cold place were the fading moments of an uneasy dream that day by day became less distinct, less likely ever to be real. For Melanie's letters would never be more than few and always shy and short on the words he needed to read.

As if through all the years of growing together she'd not clearly seen him. And that he had lived day by day with a reflection of a girl, perhaps a projection on a screen, alive only until the operator turned off the machine.

Nothing remained of Melanie except a deeper loneliness than Geoffrey had supposed life to be about. The theatre really had become dark. Everyone had gone home, leaving Geoffrey on his own, no more with the wonder of Melanie in the bright light.

If the Japanese came to where she was . . .

There was no way he could think it through.

But, even if Melanie remained safe and well, Geoffrey knew his own day had come and gone.

Other young fellows would be closing in.

Already they'd be saying, "Geoffrey's gone!"

They'd been waiting only on the opportunity.

But, at last, like Geoffrey, one by one, the turn of each to leave for war would come. And Melanie would be left to go on and on, perhaps, in the end, to learn about being alone, a thought that saddened Geoffrey greatly, for he wished her no unhappiness and no harm.

7. Aeroplane for Angels

Will gave a start, as if a presence had drawn near, as if it had passed and softly called his name.

Impossible. Except for some weird aircraft without slipstream or sound. Say an aeroplane for angels. A form of aircraft he mightn't want to know about.

His eyes opened to a rush of sickness.

Nothing on the roof suggested such a presence, but something registered just the same.

A figure, as if seen through frosted glass, for smoke from the chimneys was swaying in drifts. A man, at a distance from the house, hand raised, as if reaching towards Will to bring attention to himself.

Yet Will might have been seeing a pin (as conceived by Jackson) bearing the legend, *Enemy Observation Post*. An imaginary pin that in some strange way had come to his mind in an imaginary map.

He squeezed his eyes shut while the sickness eased, then looked out through a narrowed screen of eyelashes and tears. Through the stinging smoke tears and the three or four real tears welling up from the fright.

He saw that Geoffrey had come.

Now everyone would know about Will on the roof. Will, caught high and dry. Will acting the goat and caught out.

The shame.

Geoffrey on the bottom terrace, a few paces in from the gate, arm raised, as if just home from a walk before dark, Will catching his eye, Will in the sky.

Will had to blink hard. Had to shake his head clear. Had to manage it without sickening himself, while Geoffrey seemed to call, "I'm with you, Will."

Perhaps the raised arm made the voice. It was something other than the human throat.

"Come on, Will? I'm waiting on you."

So he swallowed back his sickness and started tightening his knees until the pressure hurt, and strengthening his grip until his chilled fingers bled, and slowly raising his free arm at the edge of a raw and abrasive breath.

Geoffrey responded with a broad sweep of fingers and palm brought edge-on to his lips.

"Be quiet," he might have said. "Let's keep it between us."

Was Geoffrey out of sight of Mum in the house?

Then, like a soldier on parade, in an exaggerated manner, Geoffrey brought himself up to attention, ramrod straight. "Sharpen up, Will!"

Was that the meaning of Geoffrey's charade, for Geoffrey rarely, if ever, made an idle spectacle of himself.

"You're not on your own, Will. Let's do this together. We'll have you down in no time."

So, might not Will reply by remaining as he was?

"Can't you see it's more than being scared? That it's like being tied. That something inside won't let me move."

Wouldn't stillness say it all? Wouldn't stillness make it clear?

"Easy for you with your feet on the ground. Me up here like you'd never understand. Hours I've been feeling the cold come on and watching the light go. You down in your cosy room. Being who you are. Being what you're going to be. Getting ready to wear your eagle wings."

Geoffrey producing a second grand sweep of the arm and bending, it seemed, to unlace a shoe, for he tossed it aside and peeled off the sock and gestured as if conveying an order.

"Off with them. Boots and socks. Off with them."

As if to say, "Of course you'll miss your footing.

Thundering great boots and a slippery roof. But it'll be worse with the dew. And worse yet when it turns to frost.

"Would you have me up there carrying you down? Would you risk being viewed from the town? Would you have everyone know that Will's not what he seems? Pull yourself together. Be a man."

Geoffrey pointing to the sinking sun and the far-off mountain ridges.

"It's like a firing squad," Will said.

Ten-league boots weighing half a ton.

Compelling his hands to go fumbling for his laces. Striving in terror to hold his balance. Going on through the motions with eyes not opening. Trying, trying to force back the sickness. Ever at the edge of falling.

Trying to wrestle off the boots with one hand, fingers of the other hooking into the sharp lip of the ridge, chilled and numbed; then afraid of looking, afraid of seeing.

Geoffrey wasn't there.

The dismay of that.

"Don't leave me, Geoffrey. Oh, my gawd, where's he gone?"

There was the head of him, as if lacking a body, leaping across the terraces as if hopping on one foot. Head and shoulders moving off to the side of the house, away from the day-living areas, beckoning for Will to move across the Private Retreat, across Will's own room, across Patricia's room, across the bath-room; Geoffrey a commanding presence conveying an overriding urgency.

"Heave—your—boots—clear!"

Geoffrey forming the words with precise lip movements.

Will whispering, "I don't know that I can. I'll throw myself with them and go falling down."

The back door slammed.

"My last call, Will. I'm locking you out."

So Geoffrey spoke aloud. "Like a crab. Two hands. Two feet. And your backside. Come on. Come on. Come on."

8. Marigolds in Buttonholes

The boots.

"What am I to do with the boots?"

He threw them as if they were never to be seen again. Two backhanded swinging throws. Two hysterical throws. The first real move of a body in terror of motion.

Making the move was the only thing. The only issue. As it had been from the start. A feat of strength far beyond ordinary life. Like lifting a house.

A prodigious effort of resolution and nerve.

It was as if everything inside him were about to

snap. Every big bone. Every little bone. Then every broken bone would break through the skin and his body would be ruined.

Between the thought and the movement he crossed a great river of great danger in roaring flood. Or he set out to cross it.

He feared he would be swept to the distant side too far downstream, far below where he wished to be, in the wrong slot of time, in the wrong country, in the wrong life.

The horror of that.

The horror of coming out in Geoffrey's life.

The fear of coming out in the life that Mum said should have been his.

He wasn't ready to be Geoffrey. He wasn't old enough to be Geoffrey. He hadn't had time to prepare.

Yet he feared there might not be a shore in wait. And there wasn't. But a bare branch waited instead and he launched himself as if dreaming, absurdly stretching for it, clawing for it, fingertips only brushing it, as if he were in the cockpit intended for Geoffrey Stevenson Houghton and had not grown enough to reach the controls or the escape hatch or the signal cartridges for stuffing in Verey pistols in critical emergencies. And all around, inside and outside, cannon shells were exploding like marigolds in buttonholes by courtesy of the happy fellows.

So Will struck the slate paving. Struck with a cry that he choked back. With a wild-eyed appeal to the slate and the house and the earth and the heavens and the all-enveloping scales of injustice.

In his moment of astonishing hurt he knew he'd broken his foot, his ankle, his shin, his knee, his hip.

He knew his leg was about to fall away in little pieces.

He lay on the paving, panting, shocked, twisted, stricken, appalled that Geoffrey had called him down without in some way being ready to receive him.

A new experience, an unimaginable pain, not only of physical hurt.

He whispered. "Oh, Geoffrey. You should've caught me. Oh, my ankle. Oh, my leg. Oh, the pain."

"Be strong, Will. You were in a jam, but you've got yourself out of it. Good show."

"You should've caught me," Will said. Then shrieked in a whisper: "Don't touch. Don't do that! You'll kill me."

"Nothing's broken," Geoffrey said, "Well, I don't think so. You've jarred yourself. Quite a jar, I'd reckon, but hardly the reason for all this fuss."

"It's broken. It's in bits. Every bone."

"Be quiet. Lean on me."

Geoffrey raised him.

"Oh, my gawd, the pain'll kill me."

"Not half as much as Mum'll kill you."

9. In the Absence of the Male

Mum looked vast, with breadth and depth and height beyond human proportions. She was such an elegant lady, but now, like a genie, her vapours filled the room.

"I'm waiting on the story, my lad. It'll need to be about the best you've ever told."

Nothing came out of Will except a meaningless mumble.

"Speak up. And look up. I'm not hearing a word."

There was nothing to hear because nothing was said. And to look up was like asking a broken reed to play beautiful music.

"Off you go," Mum said. "Until I have an explanation, you can wallow in the mess you call a bedroom."

"You can see he's upset, Mum," Geoffrey said.

"So am I upset. By his immature and improper behaviour. If we have expectations, we have them. He demeaned himself. Disgraced himself. And you, Patricia, your mantle of dewy-eyed innocence becomes more inappropriate and impossible to believe."

"I don't know what you mean, Mum."

"I wonder if there's another mother sesently fuffering confinement to the filial miseries of this planet who hears this tale as often as I? Of course you know what I mean."

"You're slipping into the spoonerisms, Mum," Patricia said.

"Don't be impertinent, if you value the sanctity of your ample bottom."

"He twisted his ankle," Geoffrey explained. "If you take a look, Mum, you'll see. He's had a bad time. He couldn't put his foot to the ground, or he'd have been back in hours ago."

Nothing that Geoffrey had to say was untrue. Creative, but not untrue; a notable act of brotherly love for a young man of high principle. Though for sisterly love Patricia would have perjured herself with every breath without fear of God or man. She changed.

Mum said, "You might have helped him in, Geoffrey, but you're not his keeper. He can speak for himself. I know from long experience he'll not suffer in silence any injury of any description, in any shape or form, yet I'm being asked to believe that he's nursed this ankle just beyond the range of our hearing for two and a quarter hours? What's wrong with his lungs? Can't he yoller? Can't he hell? Can't he crawl? Can't he buffle on his shottom?"

"Mum—when you sprained an ankle—remember?"

"We're not recalling my misfortunes, Geoffrey. We're discussing his misdemeanours. If the child elects for silence he incurs the penalty. I called him repeatedly, did I not? Am I to be known as the town crier? As the shrill on the hill? Patricia, fix him a towel and a bowl of cold water. As cold as he can stand. And then colder! And he can soak his smelly little foot in his own company for the rest of the evening. There are limits, you know. No one but the mother could endure the child. And when one comes to the plural, to the generation of the accumulation of errors that one calls the human family, the singularity of the mother becomes an incomprehensibility. The stupidity of the universal mother alone ensures the continuity of the race. I serve notice, and I nail the notice to the wall. On this little acre one goes so far and no farther. The farthermost point has been exceeded. End of performance. Fall of curtain. To bed, you wretch."

Geoffrey thought she was magnificent, though she'd driven him to distraction for much of his life.

While Patricia was of the opinion that if she attained

to half the stature of her mother she'd not be wasting it on a family like this one.

The pity was Dad missed Mum's most eloquent orations. The pity was he didn't even know, because he provoked them by his absence and her genius was wasted upon adolescents who but rarely comprehended to the full the quality of the privileges they enjoyed.

Will said this later. More than forty years later. To me.

The main complication resulting from Will's misadventure at first appeared to be a need "to get back up there again," on the ridge.

In strictest private, Geoffrey said (in an undertone, no one in the house to overhear and no observers present except Anvil on the end of the bed and a singing blackbird on a bare bough outside): "When the pilot crashes, Will. Allowing for the good news that he's still mentally and physically able, he gets back up there again. With the minimum of delay. It's a job you've got to do, little brother. Like the pilot. As soon as the swelling goes down and you're out of this bed. Or I'll have failed you at an important time."

"I'm not a pilot," Will said.

"So you'd have one rule for the Air Force and another for the Army?"

Will thought it was a terrible thing for a loving brother to say.

10. Standing Order No. 1

When news reached Will that the Japanese Second Army was marching in to lay siege to Hadden—the second week of August 1942—the ridge came to be called the Citadel.

This item of intelligence was classified Top Secret. In Will's mind this implied that associated information must never be committed to paper and never spoken aloud.

As a consequence, news of the Citadel would not come to the eyes or ears of the enemy within the gates.

* * *

An appropriate definition of *citadel*:

A smaller or inner fortified place, usually upon the heights; a fortress within a city, keeping the city under scrutiny, hence able in time of peace to discipline and govern the city and in time of war to command its loyalty and protect it.

In due course Will went on to write Standing Order No. 1 in his head. Then, scrupulously, to keep it there. In his opinion there was no other safe place for it to be.

Standing Order No. 1 didn't come easily to Will. Even before he declared to himself that at last he had phrased it reasonably well, it began to acquire an existence of its own, with new meanings almost every time he thought of it.

Looking at life as a whole, it had to be the most dangerous objective he ever required of himself, for years later it brought him directly to the proposal for the radical shift in the defence policies of his party and of his country. These he fought for and achieved, without compromise, standing alone then as he stood alone now.

Additional definition of one further item relating to 1942 only.

The enemy within the gates:
Marjorie Stevenson Houghton.

Old Pop Houghton, well-respected founder of the family fortunes, which derived from his heroic labours on the North Queensland goldfields during the 1870s, allowed himself some of the affectations of the newly rich. And, as the erudite wife of one of his grandsons subsequently put it, jolly well enjoy them he jolly well did.

Historically, Pop saw no reason why the House of Hanover in London should continue unchallenged and largely unquestioned to amass rooms full of ermine and acres full of art. And morally he saw no reason, after centuries of dry bread and water, why the House of Houghton, formerly west of Plymouth, Devon, and now north of Cairns, Queensland, shouldn't proclaim to a modest degree that it had acquired a few trifles.

Some of the affectations, like waxed moustaches, perished with Old Pop. Others, like superbly embroidered mosquito nets imported from Kashmir, perished in the tropics in his own lifetime from the saddening effects of humidity. Among surviving artefacts were the squeaking clock of magnificent aspect that came to bear his name, and the walking stick used by him to complement his top hat and to defend his august personage against common rowdies and ruffians in the streets.

The walking stick.

A handsome device of ebony and gold-plated brass. Black ebony formed the shaft. The gold-plated solid-brass handle, a likeness of the head of the sacred ibis, was able also to serve as the business end of a useful weapon, as Pop demonstrated one October evening in 1894 in Roma Street, Brisbane, when a bully-boy armed with a log of wood attempted to capture Pop's drawstring moneybag and assorted items of value. The bully-boy was swept unconscious from the scene on a stretcher.

Learned Counsel for the battered bandit later declared:

"The response to the incident alleged to have occurred near the cab rank in Roma Street on October 12 was out of all proportion. What evidence have we that a felony was in the mind of the accused except the word of his accuser? Take account of the physical condition of my client. The brutal attack upon him by this coarse fellow in the witness stand constitutes criminal intent to commit grievous bodily harm. I say the wrong man stands accused."

"And I say," bellowed the Magistrate, "that you will conduct yourself with propriety in my Court. You have a bat in your legal belfry, sir. The aggrieved citizen is a well-respected gentleman of property from the North, visiting this city on lawful business, and you will address him accordingly with proper and immediate apologies or remove yourself from my Court."

For a number of days after his rough descent from the ridge, Will was not able to get about, even to the bathroom, unless Geoffrey held him up. An acute embarrassment, for Will was a modest lad. Well into the third week he still was leaning heavily on the gold-plated handle of the ebony walking stick left in perpetuity to Will's branch of the family by their well-respected ancestor.

Six weeks of trauma, stoically endured almost without complaint, were to pass before he began to make his way around with comfort.

"Lucky you," the doctor said on the night of the accident. "Lucky your foot's not smashed up."

The doctor was so old he was beginning to go grey. He had bags under his eyes. There was a bulge of distinction centred above his tightly-drawn belt.

"You assert that these injuries occurred when you tripped over a tree root. What tree root do we have in mind? The banyan root at a lofty elevation? No banyans here."

He peered in the direction of Geoffrey and Patricia, as if he might have left his spectacles at home.

Geoffrey's eyes remained downcast. Patricia gestured with a shrug.

So the doctor went on to say:

"Lucky his ankle's not broken. Lucky about his leg. Lucky he's got a head left on his shoulders. Lucky, my lad, it seems to me, that you retain a neck intact. Or else you're a stoic like no stoic I'd wish to entertain. Lucky you, your mother's been called to the phone, so we escape the need to discuss in her presence how you came to acquire these disablements. Lucky you,

I've got twins to deliver any minute and my dinner's going cold. If I rush out now and leap into my Chevy I'll be gone, with a bit of luck, before your mother's off the phone. And you'd better suffer this inconvenience phlegmatically, actively discouraging your mother from calling me again or we may be compelled to discuss causes instead of effects. Unless, my lad, it's more than an inconvenience and you really need me. I remind you of the sorrow that lies in the desert called stoicism and stupidity."

Will sat on the last step of the lowest level of the bottom terrace. To be out of hearing and out of sight. To be alone.

Getting down there was a journey.

Getting back up might become an expedition.

Perhaps Old Pop Houghton, the ancestor, not the clock, could have been somewhere handy. Would anyone of his energy *really* lie peacefully in the grave while Will held the head of the sacred ibis and was in need? But Old Pop materializing here in the terrible cold? That might be more than ectoplasm could stand. Had he worked his passage in 1863, nineteen weeks in that appalling ship, for the agony of haunting his great-grandson in the lee of the snows?

Geoffrey said, "What are you doing here? You'll get pneumonia."

Geoffrey would have to be Pop's accredited representative.

"I'm doing nothing," Will said, "except minding my own business and suffering phlegmatically."

"You might have to do more than that about it, you know."

"Not if I follow doctor's orders. Have you ever tried suffering phlegmatically? It's enough."

"I was thinking about later. About not too much later."

"And I'm thinkin' you'll have to make yourself clearer or make yourself scarce or amuse me with a humourous recitation or a song and dance."

"The ridge. You'll have to get back there, you know."

"Ridges are for birds. I don't think you like me. I think you're trying to wipe me out."

"You know that's not true, soldier."

"Haven't you done enough damage? Letting me miss the tree. Having nothing soft for me to land on. Not even your head. You can't be serious about sending me up there again. I'm no good to you dead. All I can leave you is me fountain pen, which has always been a terrible disappointment. I think it must've been a reject."

"When the pilot crashes, Will . . ."

"You wouldn't repeat an idiotic thing like that! It's a terrible thing for a brother ever to have thought of. But to say it out loud and to say it twice!"

"If the pilot survives. If he's physically and mentally able. And as soon as he's able."

"The very same words. I saw the very same movie."

"It's a matter of nerve. And not losing nerve has nothing to do with movies. Wriggle out of something like this and you'll be wriggling out of one thing after another for the rest of your life."

"That bloomin' doctor. If he'd cut my throat it would've been an act of kindness. Who puts his head in the fire twice?"

"It's not a fire."

"Looks like one to me."

"I'm telling you, Will. Like the pilot. As soon as it's stuck together. This bit of fibre or whatever it is that you're making all the fuss about. And as soon as you're able to try. You can't expect me to go away from you feeling I've let you down."

"I'm a soldier," Will said, "not a pilot."

"I remember asking you if there was to be one rule for the Air Force and another for the Army?"

Will moaned—though not on the outside. Moaned again on the inside.

Suffering phlegmatically was enough to go on with. It really was.

But being a stoic was deadly.

So in his head, in bed and at the table and sitting over his lessons, time after time after time, day after day, Will went on working at it until it was right:

Defence of the Great City:
Standing Order No. 1.

He'd hardly brought it into line, hardly had time to express it concisely in military terms, before news reached him that the Japanese Second Army was marching up the valley with siege engines. Coming like a great host, the people in Will's head said. Stretching out of sight, as if they'd be coming on forever.

Coming with thousands of camels.

Provocative and challenging that they'd gone for the historical approach with the weapons of the last three thousand years to choose from. Everything from broken fingernails to Mitsubishi dive-bombers.

11. Lady Under Protest

Patricia Warren Houghton.

Sturdy, as in furniture built for rough-and-ready use.

Broad-shouldered, strong of arm, robust of thigh, and solid in the shank like a workaday table. This from a lifetime of exercising in deep coral sand, strong tides, and salt-water rivers, the occasional habitat of crocodiles.

Soundly put together.

Tall and supple and agile and swift from years of

tennis played under a tropical sun in the company of boisterous boys and vigorous young men.

Lean; but not in the sense of lightness or slenderness.

Hard. Healthy. Hearty. As bronzed as a well-polished plank of silky oak.

A kind of rudimentary goddess, as might be worshipped with cautious respect by physical-fitness devotees.

Confident. Assertive. Sure of her position of strength.

Ever ready to dispute an unfair decision even if awarded in her favour.

Ever ready to concede a fair point even against her own score.

An all-round good type in the experienced opinion of most.

Ever ready to defer to Geoffrey the gentleman's privilege of allowing her to take the softer chair, or allowing her to pass through the doorway ahead of him, or allowing her to grope for the largest chocolate in the bottom of the bag.

Ever ready to defer to Will, the eager beaver, the right, if demanded, of first attempt at any hazardous enterprise, such as climbing slippery roofs or falling from them. Not that she feared hazardous enterprises. To the contrary, the sisterly concession in Will's favour was generously granted to meet his continuing need to show off.

The only young male known to her not given to frequent and blatant showing-off was Geoffrey. Geoffrey managed his showing-off with subtlety. Ageing males over twenty-five—who might have wearied of leaping into murky rivers infested by crocodiles or hurling their motorcycles along mountain roads at a hundred miles an hour—failed to enter these calculations. As a consequence, males over thirty, in Patricia's judgement, were old. Those over forty were ancient. Those over fifty were dead.

Patricia was not blessed with the feminine graces.

You can't have everything, she said.

Nor was she endowed with aspects of engrossing interest to romantically inclined adolescent lads of her former acquaintance, except as a challenging companion for fast tennis, cliff-climbing, rough-water sailing, or cross-country running through tropical rain forests.

Educated by correspondence, under the dry and dour supervision of her mother.

Hence, very well educated indeed. Exceptionally so. As were her brothers.

But ever under a shadow of anxiety that Mum might lose interest or patience or more likely her temper and come to the conclusion that a college for young ladies in a doubtless distant city might *feminise* her. However unlikely in practical terms this impractical hope might seem to be. As Mum put it, the process of shared education (as distinct from education in isolation), shared discipline, shared day-by-day routine, and the shock of hour-by-hour comparison with young ladies of equal birth but infinitely greater elegance, might compel her to acquire a finish, a polish, a sorely-needed shine.

Well, at least a low-level sheen. A kind of subdued semi-matte.

Thus to provide her with a less repulsive exterior to the slight relief of the more discriminating world.

Dare we, asked Mum, console ourselves with a tolerably hopeful real-life expectation from these furious flights of our fancy?

Is it conceivable, asked Mum, as in the wilder moments of our speculation, we may eventually find ourselves with a part-polished product suitable for offering, if not for actual merchandising, at the less demanding levels of the marriage market? In the manner of a part-finished knotty-pine washstand from a cut-price store at the bottom end of town?

PATRICIA STEVENSON HOUGHTON: GUARANTEED RAIN-FOREST CEDAR. GLUED AND MORTICED JOINTS. REASONABLY EXPECTED NOT TO WARP, SPLIT, OR SPLINTER. MAY NEED APPLICATIONS OF BEESWAX TO MAINTAIN AN ILLUSION OF FINISH. NO REASONABLE OFFER REFUSED. FINANCIAL ASSISTANCE TO APPROVED CLIENT.

To wit, a finishing school for this raw, rugged, and unruly product.

An illogicality, added Mum.

If not an impossibility, added Mum.

Can one pass off a rough-hewn bench of colonial origin as a Sheraton table?

Let us suggest, for example, St. Augustine's Church of England Ladies College, located at that celebrated address close to the City of Melbourne.

Did you say finishing school?

Howled Patricia.

You mean the snaring, the trapping, the taming, the life-long captivity of Patricia.

You mean the wrapping-up of the left-overs and the hygienic disposal of Patricia.

You mean her dead end!

You give me the tearings.

Continued to howl Patricia.

You're presiding over the demolition of my human edifice.

Patricia Warren Houghton; aged fifteen years and ten months, resident at Hadden but a few weeks, and Mum, with one vigorous stroke, painted her out of the local scenery five days before the next busload of trainee fighter pilots (excellent types like Geoffrey, Dad called them) arrived to enjoy the hospitality at the pub and to dazzle the girls and their mothers at the barn dance later.

However, the foiled glitter of anticipation in Patricia's eye was subsequently found to have been an early fancy of no enduring importance. As were her mother's droll expectations of the marriage market. Hence, in 1951, the brilliant Patricia, aged twenty-four, barely out of medical school, and virtually single-handed, established a small hospital in the tribal high country of a South Pacific island.

This successful humanitarian ideal continues to develop under her administration to this day.

12. Occupied by a Foreign Power

Will, clinging to sleep, addressed the day. "I'm in seclusion, don't you know? Depart and entertain yourself some other way." Deny the day an entry, and events waiting like leopards in trees would be cheated of their prey.

The day placed a hand upon his shoulder and Will tried to shake it off. Allow it to begin and it would become the day for Patricia to go away.

At some future date an odd-looking person with a hair-set and manicured nails might return for a weekend from time to time. An alien. Like a monster with several heads. A young lady with airs and graces. Noting wear and tear on the doormat. And dust on the furniture. With a haughty manner in the bathroom. ("Out. Out.") With a horror of human odours and of family attitudes to hygiene. With a disinterest in young brothers. With a disdain of the modest pub and of the barn dance afterwards and of everything associated with the house called Hadden.

As if some strange creature had possessed Will's Patricia. As if she'd been occupied by a foreign power.

In his half-wakefulness there was nothing that he did not foresee accurately.

Will the Prophet. Will the Seer.

In his half-sleep it was as if something beyond price was about to be taken from him. Something so sacred he'd never exercised the custodian's right of opening the box to view the treasure within, and now was unable to describe it when the gods put the question: "If you don't tell us what you've lost, how can we help you recover it?"

"I think I've lost my Patricia."

"What manner of object is this Patricia?"

"You're the gods. You ought to know. She's still in the box."

He couldn't escape the hand upon his shoulder. He couldn't shake it off.

"Get yourself up, boofhead. Don't be mean. We're losing time. Don't you hear?"

Despair fell upon him like the forest full of leopards.

"It's Monday, Will. It's the day. I've got to go. You've got to get yourself out of there."

The separation would be like a death.

Will had never had to face separation from Patricia for more than a few days and dreary days they'd been.

He reached up and clung to her hand.

So they went down to the morning train: Mum, Patricia, Geoffrey, Will. Will limping on Pop's walking stick, with a bag to occupy his other hand, to convey to Mum the idea that there wasn't any pain and that the stick was a piece of nonsense. Geoffrey mooching along with the rest of the luggage as if finding a way on his own. Mum rugged up almost absurdly, dressed to travel, as if to the Pole, to present Patricia at school, and then to devote what remained of the day to the pleasures of town.

She'd be painting it red, she said. It'd be going down to history as Marjorie Stevenson Houghton Day, for celebration annually with riotous living.

She'd be home sometime, she said. On the evening train. But not today!

You're not totally incompetent, she said. Nor are you of any great interest to the criminal classes, alive, dead, or detained. Unlikely to be held for ransom, because, as everyone knows, every penny we possess I spend upon clothes. There's a shotgun in the cupboard, a meat cleaver in the pantry, rat poison in the laundry, and a cat asleep in front of the kitchen stove. One or the other should equip you to deal with all calamities likely to occur, other than flood, fire, or volcanic eruption.

If you require me, she said, to put out the fire or hold back the flood or sit upon the volcano, try phoning the Windsor. But, my chicks, my little ones, my adored offspring, refrain from reckless occupations and rash recreations. Resolve not to need me. Take your meals at the hotel or buckle your girdles about you and open the tins of lovely sardines in red oil that we've owned for years and years. So ripe they are. So redolent, they'll lend a radiance to your eye and a crinkle to your hair and oblivion to your state of mind.

Will waved goodbye to the tragic face of his sister at the carriage window.

It was unimaginably awful.

They'd known for a time that the parting had to come. The no more growing up together. The division into separated lives. But this was not to be noticed later with faint surprise. It came now, like the blow of an axe.

Geoffrey waved slightly, slowly, and only from the wrist. (*I heaved a heavy breath,* he wrote in his diary, *that no one heard.*) Geoffrey, too, was witnessing the closing of a door. Door after door for Geoffrey. More doors than Will knew about then. And Geoffrey wasn't twenty yet.

Then Patricia was gone to school; just as Will himself in the new year would have to do.

* * *

"No, Mum, No. Not school. Oh, hell. Oh, gawd . . . "

"Your language. Your language."

"If you send me to school, you'll be left on your own."

"So what? So what? The vanity of the child."

"All of us gone. What'll you do with yourself?"

"What did I do before you came? You're the one who needs companionship and interaction with people of your own age. Or you'll be a misfit."

"You're my companion, Mum."

"I'm your mother. And until now your teacher. Never your companion."

Geoffrey and Will took the hill home from the railway station in silence. Nothing ever was to be said between them about the nature of separation. Communications of the kind were oblique or silent.

Geoffrey went on through to his Private Retreat, not looking aside or back, and shut the door, shut everything out. And leant there for a while. And eventually poured a small quantity of rich brown sweet sherry and turned the crystal glass against the light (not a ritual, but performing it as if it were), closing one eye, puckering his brow, and giving another heavy breath. Then, like a great fighter ace, like the great Truscott perhaps, just out of the cockpit, just down, fatigued, pale, tense, with the glaze and glory of another combat fought and probably won, tossed it off at a wide-eyed gulp.

After the eight o'clock news, thin cigar glowing, Geoffrey started playing *Scatterbrain* on his gramophone. Playing it over and over. In his mind trying to hold close to Melanie on their only night out after loving each other for three years.

For three years a love story lived on public view. Endearments whispered. Conversations, year after year, in undertones, conveyed almost silently, almost invisibly.

Never out of sight of parents or chaperones or young children rejoicing to carry tales.

Never together, away from others, except for difficult short minutes snatched as if shared on level crossings as express trains were about to rush through.

Then a travelling open-air cinema close to home and unexpectedly the parents gave ground.

A black night of brilliant stars. All sources of light shielded from the eyes of hostile aircraft with heavy tarpaulins that could catch the wind with a startling crack. The nearby presence of the warm and secret sea. The wind foiling the mosquitoes and surging in the palms. Nature giving Geoffrey and Melanie a break.

It was *Scatterbrain* that lived afterwards in the mind.

"We're allowing this because you're leaving," Melanie's mother said. "It's for you, Geoffrey. You mightn't see her again. We know what it means. We really do. We ask you not to be hard on her if she leaves you out on a limb. She's so young."

Now nothing real was left. Only the darkness when the screen went blank at the end of the film.

The door to the Private Retreat remained shut, with Will on the outside. Alone. Like everyone else.

After a time, he looked in on Patricia's room.

The bed was disordered, the wardrobe ajar, several drawers of the cedar chest were open, and easier entry to the room might have been achieved several feet above the floor.

The familiar chaos was almost more than Will could bear and he leant his brow against the windowpane while his breath made mists on the glass.

Rain was on the mountains, coming in, and the blackbird and his nut-brown mate were busy with beak and claw, darting about the scraggy garden bed at the edge of the terrace, as if bent upon dredging it for the stuff the world was made of. Will had to go away.

He propped himself against the inside of the bath-room door, and, tit for tat, snibbed the lock to keep Geoffrey out. Then sat on the edge of the bath and cried into a towel for about an hour.

A time came when the need to wash his face and comb his hair became as important as the need for fresh air.

He limped down to the post-office store through drizzling rain, intending to spend a few pence on a chocolate bar. Something with coconut in it. By the time he was there, chocolate was gone from his mind.

The mail.

Three manila envelopes marked *On His Majesty's Service*. Two were familiar, regular, and appropriately large; workbooks returned from the correspondence school. The one addressed to Patricia coming for the last time, adding to his misery.

For Geoffrey; a different kind of letter, a slip of a letter, on the Service of His Majesty in another way.

"Oh, gawd," Will said, while the postmistress peered through the grille.

"Yes, William?"

He was trying to remember the way to the door. *"On the same day as Patricia,"* he said. *"It's not fair."*

"What's not fair?"

There's nothing, Mum had said at another time, that the postmistress needs to know that she's not learnt for herself by examining our mail against the light.

"You were saying, William?"

"I was talking to myself."

"You know what they say about people who talk to themselves! You should've covered your head. Get a chill in it and you'll be talking to yourself night and day. And wear a coat, my boy. Limping round the way you are. Get a chill in your leg and you'll know all about it. And take note, if you don't mind. Wet mail reflects badly on my office. Keep it dry."

Going back up the hill, Will had trouble with just about everything. With the blustering wind. With the rain. With his leg. And with visions of fog and fire and mountains and little aeroplanes.

"Geoffrey!"

Will dripping, drooping, tapping at Geoffrey's door.

Silence within. No opera and no *Scatterbrain* and no morning radio. No murmuring voice. No memorising of the subject of study elected for the time of day.

"Geoffrey. A letter."

He thought he heard Geoffrey clear his throat. No doubt at all that he heard a sigh. "But it won't be from her?"

"The Air Force, Geoffrey."

"You'd better bring it in, then."

"I can't. You've turned the key against me."

"That's not kind. That's not kind at all."

The door opened to a minor shock: a fug of cigar smells and sherry smells and a hint of a perfume Will might have noticed after Melanie had gone from a room.

There was a flush to Geoffrey's cheeks. Even a wildness. He might have been crying. As Will had been. As unlikely as it seemed. He might have been beating his knuckles into his brow. (*Yes,* said his diary. *Knuckles into my brow.*)

"Geoffrey. I think it's the one."

"Meaning?"

"You know the one I mean."

Geoffrey stood as if trying to bring something to

mind. Then said, "Make yourself at home, soldier. The door wasn't locked against you or against anyone. Fill a chair, why don't you? Or go get a towel. You're wet. Is it raining out there?"

Yet he opened the letter with his usual preciseness on the serrated edge of the silver-handled cheese knife inherited from the Grandfather Stevenson whose name he bore. (A gift to Grandfather from a lady he'd loved.)

"Yes," Geoffrey said, "it's come." And sat heavily on the edge of the unmade bed.

Then later: "The call-up."

And yet later: "Pour me a drink, Will. A little drink, Will. A celebration. I can't catch myself pouring it, can I? Having one aboard already. A subtlety, Will. I hope it's not the signal of a weakness. I couldn't stand being a drunk. Couldn't live with myself. But you never know about yourself, do you? Do you mind?"

"Of course I don't mind."

"Pour two. One for you."

"Mum'd kill us if I did."

Geoffrey's smile was thin. "Have you been taking a shower? You haven't dried your hair."

In another minute or two, he said, "Come on, Will. Do the honours. Please . . .

"And where's our mother? And what was her fond farewell? Get lost, my chicks, until my return, this year, next year, never.

"And where's my Melanie who doesn't care?

"And my father up some creek somewhere, tuned like a reflex to the wishes of Southern Command?

"Mutual love and support. The essence of the family, Will. Everyone holding everyone else up.

"So I'm proposing—I really am proposing—to become modestly alcoholic. Thus, I hope, modestly insensitive to the anguish of the world. It really is my first such degeneration, I swear. But I fear I was on the way before you stepped inside and delivered the perfect excuse. Forgive me if you can, little brother. I may need a little care before I'm through.

"We're all we've got, you know, you and me. Patricia's gone for good and all, I fear. And that, Will Houghton, is not really the best of British luck for you.

"Do go dry your hair before you catch a chill. When you come back, I'll still be here, for a week or two."

13. Top Secret

The strategy of the defence of Hadden, in the course of the siege imposed by the Japanese Second Army, depended upon the application of Standing Order No. 1.

Never, during Will's struggle to get the extraordinary thing straight in his head, did he grasp the nature of what was going on. Yet down some back alley of his mind a voice warned him. *Beware. This mightn't be a little-boy game.*

In adult life the warning came true and Will could scarcely carry the weight of it. The words were fitting situations he'd never dreamt of. Geoffrey had left a yoke for him to wear, to bear, for the rest of his life.

Had Geoffrey been predicting there'd never be an easy way for Will Houghton? That he'd be forced always to choose the hard way as an act of remembrance? Even when it hurt. Even when it invited self-destruction. Geoffrey not only predicting it, but making it certain.

Geoffrey might not have inferred or intended anything of the kind. He might never have possessed the subtlety or the wisdom. It might have been Will himself all the time.

Standing Order No. 1 assumed the stature of an unwritten command that Will would never be able to tear up and scatter to the wind. How often he wished he'd not drummed it into his brain as Geoffrey had drummed Air Force facts and figures into his brain.

Life might have been different if he'd written it down. Then he could have labelled it less than Top Secret. Could have called it Confidential. Could have said it was a draft and revised it out of existence. Could have scrapped the terms *most lofty point* and *Citadel* and *place of command* and *Great City*. Could have called each by its proper name and left no room for interpretation. Then he could have ignored the idea that he was sworn to a life of honour and walked away and forgotten it, as others walked away from obligations and forgot them. If, in the first place, it hadn't mattered, it couldn't matter later.

No other person knew the order existed. (No one, until Will told it to me.) No one would have cared if it stopped existing. If the world had known, much of the world would have shrugged it off.

("Honour over such a matter? My dear man. You can't be serious.")

But cheating on Geoffrey was forbidden. Cheating on William Stevenson Houghton was forbidden, too.

God Save the King.
Defence of the *Great City*.
Classification of Document: Top Secret.
Standing Order No. 1:
The most lofty point shall be called the Citadel.
Officer in Charge shall establish his place of command in the Citadel.
Officer in Charge shall observe daily from the Citadel and at a quiet time determine the nature and disposition of the enemy and by this action foil the enemy.
Officer in Charge shall not deviate, even when the tactical situation is hazardous; for example, enemy shock troops are active within the gates. Extreme caution is an obligation of command, but the contract shall remain in force until the last battle falls silent and victory is accom-

*plished and all objectives are honourably
achieved.*

Thus Will laid down his rules for life and became the
servant of his gift for language developed at his mother's feet.

14. Surprise Attack

Thursday, third day of spring, third day of September.
The day nominated by Will for honouring the unspoken promise to Geoffrey. Now gone. Now gone away.

Morning glow was on the blind, along with shadows thrown by twigs; making words and mysteries like the writing on Nebuchadnezzar's wall in Babylon. As if the blind were a message pad for the entertainment of a god bent on manipulating the sun.

Your contract is the Citadel and the day has come.

"Half of it I concede," Will thought. "Half of it I don't. You go write on someone else's blind or I'll send it crashing for the ceiling. If you get your sticky fingers caught, bad luck, mate."

Will lying there worrying, trying hard to stop the day from happening; a quaint and futile flaw of character that in all his life he never overcame but once.

The blackbird singing like an angel outside. A striking accomplishment on a stomach so full of friends and neighbours. An angel from a slightly disreputable heaven.

Perhaps the squawking youngsters in the family tree had left home for the day to visit Great-aunt Chloris in the she-oak at the distant corner of the Houghton kingdom, and thankfully, gratefully, the master of the terrace had an interval to call his own.

In human terms, a reasonable hour for abandoning bed, sunrise occurring a little earlier.

Will adrift on his back, afloat a restless sea, attempting to stare glassily into a mystic zone of no focus above his head, making a point of avoiding the window glow, still trying to lose the hour, the day, and the prospect of the day, in a maze of words and phrases learnt from a lifetime of listening to Mum.

In time Will stretched with all his might to build the skill, to wield words and phrases disarmingly, with irony, like dance, or like songs.

Now he stared into his private fog as if he had spent the night with eyes raised in adoration of the sagging ceiling where aged water stains and spiderweb wisps and mildew spots made maps and charts in the Jackson manner, as well as a minor work in progress by Michelangelo. Now it seemed that Will was committed to serious consideration of every imaginable reason why he should spend the day doing nothing else.

Significantly, Hadden was at present surrounded by hundreds of siege engines, Trojan horses, warlike gentlemen in strange clothing marching round the walls blowing trumpets, cavalry units mounted upon camels, battering rams, Big Bertha guns on railway bogies, Panzer divisions, and fiendish chemical weapons bubbling in fragile test tubes clasped in the clumsy hands of rank upon rank of short-sighted soldiers wearing glasses, all in constant danger of tripping, all afire with enthusiasm to die for the Emperor. Then, from time to time, like a winged dragon, a single-engined Mitsubishi or Nakajima, code-named Zero or Kate, came in low through St. Sebastian's Gap disguised as a Wirraway with a yellow sash.

Thus the enemy multitudes controlled Hadden until Will could bring Standing Order No. 1 into effect and freeze them into tactical disarray. (The latter phrase from Jackson, *Siege Warfare*, Volume 2, Chapter 8.) In the meantime, there being no object in view for Will's day except the dreaded assault upon the Citadel, from which only the Supreme Powers could spare him, by sending earthquake, flood, or fire.

But first there'd be the obligatory lessons, if he were not to grow up a moron. Over which Mum might or might not preside. Depending upon the use she made of her own day at its points of collision with Will. Upon whether she pursued her impulse of the night before to bend her back in the garden—because spring had come—or to act upon the more inviting fancy of catching the morning train. Well, she said, it might be inappropriate spending the momentous third day of September stooped in a defenceless attitude in the midst of a cruel uprising of rampant green growth, when for the sake of a mere seventy miles there and back she could enjoy the sales in the lovely concrete city.

Then for Will (whichever choice Mum made) there'd be the breathtaking excitement of breakfast, lunch, and dinner, Mum having of late lost her wild creative urges in the kitchen. There being no one to cook for anymore. This information, conveyed with a shrug, adding much to the morale of Will's regiment.

Bed went on feeling better all the time, though waking up with a foul disease, granted by some minor deity with a morbid interest in striking humans deaf, dumb, or blind, would have simplified proceedings. Like being prostrated from a raging pimple or a relapsed limp or sudden senile decay.

Waking up hale and hearty on the morning of battle was a fatal condition, as any soldier could tell you.

Unhealthy people had no idea how fortunate they were, lying in bed out of harm's way.

Well, he could hold his breath until he half-suffocated and lapsed into a coma. Though picking the moment to stop would be crucial, or the happy fellows would be marching in rubbing their hands in anticipation of making a further generous contribution to the widows and orphans tax.

Half-starving, by comparison, appealed strongly as a superior way. Except that he was always half-starved and no one would spot the difference.

Half-dead, then?

Old age, the best-known reason for being half-dead, was difficult to arrange in a hurry.

The awful problem unresolved, Will came to realise that his half-seeing stare had drifted into territory occupied by a hairy huntsman spider about six inches across the beam. This well-endowed character appeared to be lodged motionless in the ornamental cornice directly above Will's head.

A most splendid specimen, undoubtedly having acquired its magnitude over years of murderous hit-and-run warfare in the bloody battles of life.

Big enough to scare the living daylights out of the creatures on the planet, lions and tigers included.

Big enough to send Will shrieking out of bed.

"Mum!"

The gods had intervened as usual, though with a touch of guile at first not in evidence.

Mum had hurried for the early train, having declined to take breakfast. No doubt she'd be heading for some favourite spot for sticky buns and hot chocolate as soon as she hit town. Leaving Will with a dreary-looking packet of wheat flakes and a can opener and the spider in unchallenged possession of the bedroom.

This, in turn, led Will to introduce Anvil to the edge of the doormat and point him into the bedroom in the right direction. "Terrorise him, boy. Rip him down, boy. Show him those needle-sharp teeth."

Anvil wriggled firmly from Will's grasp, returned to the kitchen, and put his nose back in the cat bowl, while Mum continued her bustling advance upon the railway station, passing unharmed through the ranks of the Japanese Second Army.

Will with a sigh felt moved to seek Anvil's opinion upon this matter also.

"Clear to see where the blighters are getting their information. Wouldn't you agree? Talk about enemy agents residing within the gates!"

Anvil had more pressing matters on his mind.

Will tried a further change of subject.

"Pussycats. Mothers. Huntsmen spiders. Two-bit tuppenny gods. All working in the one direction. All shoving me up onto the roof. All ordering me to occupy the Citadel. No one lendin' me a hand. You'll only have yourselves to blame when I get stuck in the barrel and die in the breach."

Anvil sat beside his bowl and washed his face.

"I reckon the message is coming through loud and clear. I reckon I'm stuck with the roof and stuck with the huntsman and probably stuck with baked beans and lumps of fatty pork in specially watered-down tomato sauce to match the tin opener for breakfast, lunch, and afternoon tea."

This was the moment for a missile of unknown origin to strike a wall or windowpane at the front of the house.

Will's heart responded with a jump that was at once followed by the squeak of the cat door at the foot of the back door at the end of the passage—as Anvil went about a cat's business.

Upon such moments are destinies shaped.

15. Fix a Tiger with Your Eye

Some might call it the first shot in the Battle of the Great City, and the key to it. Others might look more to the events of the ridge, or to Geoffrey's diary. In Will's view, all was a wonderful unity of many sadnesses.

He questioned the sound of impact with a flash of anxiety, but then layers of thought started breaking like waves within him, each distinct, as if visible to him, like multiple images appearing upon a single frame of photographic film in a developing solution.

Nothing like it had happened to him at any other time. The unforgettable sharpening of a distinctive talent that in later years he'd relive in times of threat or challenge. The sound of impact again. The brain-storm again. And swift responses to repulse his enemies.

The Japanese Second Army . . .

They'd been sitting there for weeks. In a manner of speaking. While stoically, as forbidden by the doctor, Will drilled himself to walk without medical super-vision.

They'd been out there playing rummy or whatever it was that entertained Japanese Second Armies while they were busy worrying besieged enemies half to death.

Suddenly blasting in with a big gun at breakfast when no one was expecting it. Well, war was war and discourtesy was just another weapon.

While the Wheaties went soggy in the plate.

Formerly making out that the attack against Had-den would come in historical terms: announced by envoys, heralded with rolling drums, and delivered from siege engines, massed camel charges, battering rams, and soldiers in breastplates and helmets.

Well, they'd gone for big guns instead and opened up dead on line, dead on range. First shell, first strike.

So . . .

If Will didn't proceed to storm the Citadel, as di-rected by the sunlight on the bedroom blind, there wouldn't be two bricks left standing by nightfall when Mum got home.

Unless the reason for the attack were to be found in her recent departure! Their inside agent, the saboteur and spy within the gates, being no longer within the gates, being out of harm's way these past seven or eight minutes and now safely in the train! So in whams the first shell like Mum slamming the door on the way out; one being the signal to load the gun for the other.

At the same time . . .

Anvil might be the issue!

Follow that cat!

Will's thoughts about likely realities; his imaginings about highly unlikely unrealities; his considerations of warfare ancient and modern; and his physical responses to each question became a single impulse, a single signal from the brain:

"The other way. The front door. Like lightning on greased skids."

Cat and human arrived within a second of each other; Anvil round by the back, Will crashing through the front with questions looking for answers.

Anvil leaping for a drift of downy feathers beneath the newly spring-cleaned window to Mum's bedroom.

A fallen blackbird lying in a scatter of soft feathers, wings stirring, as if drawing its last breaths, Anvil leaping for possession.

"No!" Will shouted, thoughts springing to the

gourmet. To the glutton. To the bird of such spirit and wickedness.

Will leapt as Anvil leapt, and met the cat with the flat of a hand, sweeping him aside.

The casualty wasn't the gourmet.

"You rotten bully," Will shrieked. "It's a baby."

Anvil sprang back and Will swept again with the edge of his hand and yelped to the strike of teeth like needles across his knuckles.

"You're obscene, cat. And stuffed to the gills with breakfast. You'd sick the poor little thing up."

Anvil's claws showed bare, and his teeth showed sharp, and he hissed his fury at the senseless interference of this human whose company and care and the foot of whose bed he considered to be his personal property.

"Scram, Anvil!"

The human who now continued to assault and offend him with threats and fists and the planting of a hand like a grid over his morning snack.

The human whose attitude was gross and ridiculous.

"A once-only benefit of the doubt, cat. If I feel your teeth again, you'll be sorry. No larrikin cat does that to me."

The human who went on throwing wicked swipes and shouting and glaring and staring and fixing a noble cat with the evil eye.

Fix a tiger with your eye.

Part of a story read by Will. Last year. Or earlier.

When the beast selects his prey.

If you'd see another day.

Fix him with your steady eye.

Fix that lion; fix that tiger.

I've done it then; I've fixed this here pussycat!

"The message, Anvil. You're a scrubber. You're fighting out of your class."

Anvil squashing against Mother Earth. Measuring his distances. Setting himself outside reach. Making rippling sounds and pointed promises to all creatures clothed in feathers or cloth and rash enough to blink both eyes.

Will's stare glinted and glared. "Beat it, mate. Bite me again and I'll sink my teeth through you like you'd never know what bit you."

Gently he grasped the young bird lying there; so limp to his touch he feared its life had gone. Warm and soft and no response to the sensitivity of his hand.

Will anxious to look. Anxious to know. But not ready to move his eye. Becoming more and more aware of another presence that would not be ignored. A shrill and remarkable bird-cry repeated without pause. Like the protest of a dry axle and a dry wheel.

Extraordinary.

The master of the terrace. The glutton. The gourmet. The consumer of friends and neighbours.

Four human paces from Will's crouched stance. On the ground. Three paces from the bristling cat. This bird at the edge of Will's vision. Prancing. Switching his tail. Screeching. Delivering a declaration:

"By all that's fair, what's happening there? What are you doing with my kid under your claw? Young human hunting with the cat like the grown-up human with the falcon and the dog. Big human bully and little blackbird."

The indignation. The spirit of the bird.

"If you'd not have that furred freak pecked blind. If you'd not have it driven nuts. Lock it up. Keep it out of the reach of me."

The passion. The stature.

Anvil, the cat with wings, twisting in the air, goaded by this feathered thing no bigger than a cat's hind leg, but the feathered thing, shrieking without pause, took to a twig: "I'll destroy you, cat. I'll have you put down. What have you done to my kid, you lousy human, you lousy cat?"

Will drew the young bird to the heat of his body and said, "I'm on your side, mate. I don't hold any brief for this lousy cat. But he's only being a cat. Like you're being a blackbird. And all he's had for breakfast is his morning bread and milk, while you've been biting off every head that wasn't quick enough away."

Explaining myself to a screeching bird? To this rogue who'd bite my head off, too, if he was big enough.

"Take a breath," Will yelled.

"Shut up and listen!

"Your kid was a rookie. She did it on her own. Her own mistake. Like a trainee pilot. Never farther than the first mistake away from the happy fellows."

A thought that Will would rather not have had.

But again to the blackbird: "She didn't *see* the window. That's got to be obvious even to a pea-brain like you. She thought it was empty air. But a window was there like a mountain in a fog . . ."

Will said to himself, "I don't like what I'm hearing."

Once more to the bird: "Shut your noise, you shrieking bird-thing. You'll never hear a word? How will I ever think? You're worse than the perishin' cat. I've seen you eating people who've lived round here for years. Birds of a feather, you and this pussycat. Fully paid-up members of the same club. The Can't-Take-Your-Own-Medicine Club. So shut up and beat it. Beat it, both of you. What I say round here, goes round here. I'm the human round here."

Will walked off almost in tears and sat himself on the bench at the front door and opened his cupped hands. Blood on his hands. Blood on the feathers.

So the tears broke the banks.

"It isn't fair . . .

"I know you can't be six weeks old. I know you'd not have grown into a brute like your father. I know you can hardly tell your front from your back. I know you've hardly stretched your poor little wings.

"It wasn't your fault flying into our awful window. How were you to know when you're only learning to crawl?"

It was Will's blood from the teeth of the cat.

"Oh, I'm glad about that."

But he went on blinking through his tears while the blackbird bore in.

No sign of Anvil. Thanks for the mercy of that.

Bright black eyes beading in. Bird wearing spectacles with yellow rims. Jigging about on the flagstones. Orange beak wide open like the mouth of a street-corner orator. Standing six inches tall. Addressing Will. Eye boring up to eye.

"It's your fault, you lousy human. Muscling in on us birds. It's your house and your window and your lousy cat. It's your responsibility to fix up my kid."

"People were round here," Will said, "before blackbirds. Thousands of years and not a sign of blackbirds. I looked it up. Your lot came out on sailing ships. In cages. Fed on board by kids like me. Blackbirds are immigrants like the rest of us."

"Rubbish," shrieked the blackbird.

"You're a Johnny-come-lately. Like the Houghtons. Making out you own the country. Making out you've got a licence to gobble it up."

The blackbird said, "I'm expecting you. I'm requiring you. I'm laying it on you."

Will said, taking in the world: "If you get hit too hard, you die. Blackbirds have got to put up with it same as us. Which is why humans run like mad to get out of the way. There's nothing I can do for your kid. If you hurl yourself at solid objects you get the brains knocked out of you or the life knocked out of you."

"It's your world," the blackbird said. "Humans made it. None of us birds had a hand in it. None of us asked to be born. We woke up and there we were. In a world full of humans and windows and walls and cats. Fix up my kid or I'll nag you out of your little mind."

In a while Will looked down again into two bright black eyes and the continuing complaint, the rapid hell-fire protest of the dry axle and the dry wheel, and the prancing and the jigging and the switching of the tail.

"We don't make birds," Will said. "We can't wind them up when they stop. The mystery's got nothing to do with us. When it's over for blackbirds, it's over, the same as for us. But I'll dig a nice little hole for your kid, because she needs it, mate.

"Don't dog me. Get off my back. I've had enough. I'm out of my depth. It's time you bothered someone else."

16. William Stevenson Houghton. Sir

More of September 3, 1942.

Thursday.

Day of the excited young blackbird. Generally of excited young blackbirds everywhere, rarely convinced that clear spaces in real life can be solid and may differ fatally from the beautiful, magical air.

A time of testing. The world over. As ever.

And initially, in the vicinity of Haddenham, Australia, of the transfer of Will from the north face of the house to the south to avoid the punishing presence of the loudmouthed glutton. This Will achieved by passing from the front external door to the back external door through the interior hallway that divided the house into unequal parts, first shutting the front door with a clout, and after an appropriate pause passing silently out through the back and creeping to the toolshed for a spade and on to the nearest rosebush.

Well, why not for a special little bird of many unfulfilled talents? Early perfecting a lusty appetite for the luckless earthworms delivered to her table by her doting parents and quickly growing the flight feathers that sent her eagerly into the world like an ill-directed arrow. The best intentions of parents sometimes producing undesired effects.

Will's decision to bury the little bird under a woody old rosebush was a sentimental error and became one of the last manifestations of his private fantasyland. Along with acting the goat on rooftops and giving misleading information to busy doctors.

But as General Jackson also was about to do, the rosebush painfully proved a point, bringing more blood to Will's wildly smarting hands and more startled tears to add to those given for the small creature so reverently placed and covered.

A tumble of words came then to Will's mind, not unrelated to those heard during the wonder of a cathedral service when he was six. Heard from a man like a king in a towering hat:

Are not five sparrows sold for a penny?

Not one shall crash into the window without God's knowledge.

Don't fret for yourself, even when life confuses you and thorns and claws are all around you.

Your value is more than a flock of sparrows.

"If you say so," Will said.

So he allowed the spade to fall and tucked his wounded hand into the pit of the other arm, and took the first step towards the house, towards the bathroom, but his sight focussed upon broken glass. Glass like a knife, like a spearhead, like a dagger, part of a box against the wall near the door. Then more. Numerous pieces, all jagged, like knives, like spearheads, like daggers, that he must've passed, though never seen, many times before.

"My gawd."

A month ago, two months ago, he'd even asked Mum what the curious object might be.

"It's a cold frame."

"What's a cold frame?"

"That's a cold frame."

"Yeh, Mum, yeh. But what do they do with them?"

"Raise tomatoes in them. Or cucumbers. Or anything you fancy early in the season that needs heat to grow. Do you wonder in a climate like this?"

"Why not call them hot frames, then?"

"The locals call them cold frames. They haven't a word for hot, my chicken."

She was a problem. Taking her almost any way at all. Literally or otherwise.

The lid of the cold frame opened upwards like a shutter. A window once upon a time. An old window frame of four panes put to another use. Now with every pane broken. All like knives. Like spearheads. Like daggers.

"Gawdfathers. And there are more of these contraptions round the corner."

Will standing as if fixed to the narrow flagstone path, closing his armpit tightly over his injured hand, only steps from the back door, looking anxiously in other directions, as if the tears of the shock of the rosebush had washed a fog from his eyes.

All around, everything was wildly overgrown. Although in a way he'd always known. But not as he saw it now. Everything having taken on a quality of change like the change of seasons. Last summer's strong straw now fragmenting, now breaking down, now crumbling into soft new grass. Drawing Will's keenest attention. Was he seeing broken bottles there? Lying broken and jagged since when? Since the colony was settled? Was he seeing the tail of a coil of barbed wire largely buried in the ground?

Will whispered, "What are these terrible things doing here?"

So it took on a further quality; that of immediate danger; as if the earth might rear up in the shape of creatures made of jagged glass and barbs of wire, all with ravening appetites for the human taste.

Will backing off. Looking for the door, disconcerted, almost guilty, as if he were the one responsible.

Getting himself into the house. Remembering the bathroom and hurrying there. Taking refuge in lashings of soap and water that washed away the dirt and the blood and a little of the danger and some of the guilt. Then he reached the iodine down and lint dressings and sticking plaster and in a minute or two made his way to the kitchen for the breakfast abandoned a time before.

Anvil, recently not thought of, was immediately found upon the table, snuffling through the bowl in which lay but a smear of Will's once soggy Wheaties.

"Oh, hell!" Will bellowed.

Anvil leaping half-way across the room at a bound; the cat door squeaking wildly an instant later.

"You stinkin', lousy cat!"

Will would have sworn to the skies if he'd been less certain the Higher Powers were not unusually close. And he'd have squashed Anvil with a brick if he had had a brick and the strength of character and the speed to catch up.

And if he hadn't been half-fainting from injuries and hunger, he'd have made up a new passage of Scripture about no cat being worth a fifth of five sparrows.

And he'd have had more to say about his elegant mother recently departed upon the morning train reading *Anna Karenina* for the third time in the last thirty years, and upon the condition of the Wheaties pack left empty.

Immediately followed by a predictable sequence of

awful events, beginning with the realization that there wouldn't be a spoonful of Wheaties, even for crunching up dry, until the grocer boy walked his bike through the gate on the morrow with his little wicker basket jammed between the handlebars. If Mum had remembered to place her order and the storekeeper had not mislaid it.

For now it was obvious that the milk jug was empty also, until the dairy farmer called at about noon to fill it from his can. If the dairy farmer remembered to call at all and remembered to bring his can. Which he didn't always, having recently celebrated a majestic birthday related to the twelfth, the twenty-fourth, and the fortieth, and acquired overnight a quaint new reputation for absence of mind. The magnitude of sixty-five years offering special privileges to an alert fellow, including special considerations about the house granted by family members who wished him to go on bringing home the bacon until he dropped, and wished him not to retire to his rocking chair, thus compelling them to seek employment. Calculated lapses of memory thus kept the family on its toes.

And no bread in Will's pantry either, even for feeding to the birds, until the baker came. If the baker's 1926 model van didn't fail to start. Or run out of petrol. Or get a puncture. Or in any of twenty or thirty other ways break down en route, five or six or ten miles distant. Or simply expire in the bakery yard, belching steam.

And elsewhere on the pantry shelf not a solitary

bean with or without lumps of fatty pork, with or without specially watered-down tomato sauce, and nothing else in evidence except the usual ageing tins with faded labels and rust stains round the edges.

The famous tins of sardines in red oil that took your breath away, tins of lobster soup, of anchovies, of smoked oysters, and of clams in the shell; jars of pear and ginger conserve, packets of gunpowder tea, and related delicacies attuned to trained—or what Patricia termed *demented*—adult taste, usually served prior to outbursts of affectionate behaviour. All having acquired such great age (during the long waits between Dad's home visits) that Mum declined to open them anymore and kept them for old times' sake. (Like the icing-sugar horseshoe and the menu from Simpson's on the Strand.) These items on the pantry shelf, even long ago when fresh, were not to Will's liking. And at breakfast the idea was nauseous. Whereas the part-eaten block of chocolate and the balance of the week's pocket money remained in his bedroom under the malevolent supervision of the gigantic huntsman.

Hence, for breakfast, cracker biscuits and too much mango chutney once cheerfully made by a lovely lady during her years of sun and song among the rustling palms.

Whereas two crisp rashers of bacon, two eggs both sides golden, and hot-buttered toast with a mug of chocolate milk might have changed the shape of history. These delights failed to reach the table, so history took its course.

Songs in the sun were not to come again readily for the Houghtons either.

But most things mend in the end, though often not at the point of breakage.

Immediately to follow, more of September 3, 1942, more of the making of the man approached with respect in later years by admirals, generals, and air marshals and addressed as Prime Minister Houghton. Sir. And an account of the fires of the Battle for the Great City that burned for three days.

17. Battle for the Great City

Will went out to face a danger that he didn't fully see. Went out with a tightness under the heart that often was there when he deeply cared.

Will went out to look for a way onto the roof that wouldn't totally terrify him and perhaps offer a soft place to fall.

He went out to honour promises never spoken, to obey orders never written, to do something positive about the Citadel that never was, and to drive back the Japanese Second Army then several thousand miles away.

Will went out with raw hands stinging. With aches

that reached from hip to foot and were like a mouthful of teeth overdue for attention. And with a bellyache from the ravages of mango chutney on an empty stomach.

("I'll get you, Mum. That huntsman, too, blockin' the way to my pocket money. You'd better bring home a bag of sticky buns or else.")

Will sighing from the weight of woes; from the mathematics of trying to keep a count of them. Even from his sadness for the little bird in the hole. And from the barbs and the daggers and the spears and the knives.

"It's good that Mum's not here. We'd be getting in each other's hair. She'd have driven me up the wall. All the time yelling no. Raising her arm and pointing her finger and making fine speeches. Today's for being on my own."

Will went out to face the numbing fear of the ridge in cold blood. A strange feeling, setting the mood to face it cold. As Geoffrey might have to do.

Geoffrey with hands cold and feet cold. Geoffrey with an all-over chill, facing what Heaven alone could tell.

So, cold meant you were scared. Meant you were afraid. Meant you'd gone ashen or pale.

No disgrace, going cold.

"I reckon heroes must be scared," Will said, "or they wouldn't be heroes. They'd only be fools. They get on with the job even though they're scared."

He went out to influence history, though not aware

of it. Never coming to appreciate fully the value of his own special place, even years on, for he was ever a modest man.

But immediately the barbs of wire reared again and the daggers of glass and it began to go wrong.

Anvil went out also. From wherever Anvil had gone into hiding.

Will looked back and there he was. Like a terrier. Though never closer than three or four paces and rarely farther than ten behind. A long-time habit. A convenience. Anvil's common-sense method of policing his territory in the company of a human presence, thus easing the risk of damage to his person from hostile cats, dogs, or old-man possums likely to dispute a boundary. There being no reason in Anvil's view why the practice should be varied because of his recent disgrace. He saw none of it as disgrace. He saw it only as irrational human behaviour, with the resumption of a working relationship the outcome of his generosity of spirit.

The blackbird was present also. From almost the first moment. And long afterwards in the laws of the land. Present in memories of such importance to Will that they influenced the child-care legislation known for a time as the Houghton Law.

Somewhere in the dust of the Earth, the blackbird slept honoured by statutes that made an effort to protect young humans from the inhumanity of their kind. Blackbird, though holding a very lofty opinion of himself, failed to foresee his surprising fame.

In the first moments of his first circuit of the house, Will discovered an unknown land and came under attack from the strident, demanding, and daring blackbird.

Almost at once, Will was shaking his head and asking incredulous questions of himself.

Jackson—like a storm—would have slapped him on a charge. Would've thrown him in the guardhouse. And in the course of a monumentally continuous breath, with suitable oaths (deleted), would've shredded Will's character thus:

"How can any soldier with ambitions for senior command live for months with hazards of this infamy at every whip and turn and ignore detail so conspicuous that a child would stand aghast. You disgrace the King's uniform and the honour of command."

Whenever the thought returned, Will burned up with shame.

And the bird, beak crammed with earthworms, went on attacking the nerves and the brain. Throughout the day. And the next day. For seventeen consecutive days. Until neither cat nor Marjorie Stevenson Houghton would venture out-of-doors. Until Will in a rage pursued the creature into his tree, up and up, shrieking, "You stupid bird. You'll put a cork in it or

I'll stuff my fist down your throat. I'll wring your neck. I'll shoot your head off with the shotgun. Go tell your wife lay another egg! Do you hear?"

He heard.

The hazards.

The hazards that would have aroused Jackson's righteous fury and that Will had failed to observe from early winter until September 3:

Tangled and thorny vegetation in dismaying depth.

Collapsing stacks of decomposing timber studded with rusty nails.

Heaps of crumbling hand-made bricks that gave way to foot pressure; Will leaping back in alarm; bricks crawling with small slow sleek satiny spiders, each infinitely more dangerous than the swift, swash-buckling, huge, and hairy huntsman.

Firewood flaking with age, split and stacked long ago, overgrown with blackberries, infested with millipedes, centipedes, slaters, and probably with snakes stupefied by cold. Infested with everything that wriggled or writhed or crawled.

Three broken cold frames jagged with knives, with spearheads, with daggers of splintered glass against the very walls of the house.

Seven sprung coils of rusty barbed wire lodged like mantraps in decomposing grass. In wait for the unwary. Will's shoulders drooping. The old sickness rising.

Broken raw-edged bottles in clusters, littered as if thrown widely in a rage.

Will dragging his feet. Beginning to limp. Dragging round and round ever more nervously, in ever greater depression.

Seeing nothing that looked like a place where he'd ever want to climb. Passing everything many times, but always seeing the same. The same nowhere to climb. Carrying a fog in his brain.

The blackbird presenting his case with scarcely a pause:

"All this stopping and starting and shuffling around won't be getting me off your back. I'm staying right where I am till you fix my kid. Us birds have got rights."

From time to time he took another tack.

"Why are you giving that cat protection? You ought to give it the toe of your boot. Why are you giving it houseroom? You ought to stuff it in a bag and chuck it in the creek."

These terrible hazards.

None given a moment's thought when he'd been rushing about with Patricia.

Not considered when he'd climbed the half-rotten trellis and the too-steep roof with the overlapping ends of metal and the projecting heads of nails and the rust disguised with cheap paint.

Not in the reckoning when he'd launched himself from the edge in despair not knowing what was underneath.

He could've severed an artery and bled to death.

Could have lost his sight.

Could've maimed himself or killed himself in the instant of the leap.

Being left with arthritic pain and a diseased hip to drag around for much of his life was getting off lightly. Though the doctor could have spared him much had he heard the truth, had he not been in haste, had he not uttered his warning about stoics, thus creating one.

Will leant against the house, short of breath, thinking of his father; thinking of an engineer buying a death trap while allegedly awake.

"Did he never check it out?

"We could've been messed up for life. Any one of us. Mum wandering about in her dream. How would Dad have gone for that? Having that on his conscience? Spoiling the look of her?

"And what of flippin' Geoffrey? Whose son does he turn out to be? Round here long enough to count the blades of grass. Long enough to clean the place up. Would've given him something to do with his time."

Will sighed.

"So whose son does that make me?

"Jackson wouldn't own me, and it's only because of him that I'm seeing it. Seeing two faces of it. Not just one. Which means someone's set me up, or I wouldn't be here on my own. How could Jackson have anything to do with that? And Geoffrey's too dumb. He's in the clouds. He's floating on feathers. Did Old Pop Houghton set me up?

"That blasted bird beating at my brain.

"Am I worried about getting myself cut up? If Geoffrey didn't give a damn, that was his business. Maybe red-back spiders and barbed wire and sleeping snakes and broken bottles and daggers of glass never even got to him. Never gave himself a thought. Or anyone else a thought either.

"That's one face. What about the other?

"Am I committed to the defence of the Great City, or am I fooling around? Am I training to be a general? Or am I having a little-boy game?

"Am I committed professionally? Am I applying myself to military problems?

"If I am, the hazards get a new name. They go on staying in place like they were set in concrete. You call them obstacles. You call them barbed-wire entanglements. You call them minefields. You call them tank traps. You call them lines of defence. Which suggests, Will Houghton, that snap judgments don't always crack the game."

He cried aloud: "Oh, to hell with the stupid game."

He sagged against the house and hung his head.

"Well, who's to say? I *do* know that Mum *doesn't* know what she's asking. I've got to be fair. And I've been thinking unfair things about her all morning.

"But always wandering about the place the way she does. Talk about aimless. Talk about a terrible waste of a fantastic lady. What's she getting round here except giving me an education and rushing off to town on the train? And I'll bet she reckons I'm a waste of effort anyway.

"How could she know about the oath of allegiance? Or the standing orders? Or the honour of the regiment?

"Which makes me the only one between here and forever who'll ever give a continental about it. I made the oath. I wrote the standing orders. I gave the promises.

"The defences are engineered. They exist. The Great City is defended. The Citadel's impregnable. Which is why the Japs haven't attacked. They knew it was never on.

"So Jackson proves a point. If the lay of the land, he says, is a problem for you, it's a problem for the other fellow. The obstacles that bar your way, bar the way of the enemy. The flood that gives you the horrors in your retreat brings your enemy later to his drowning and defeat.

"Oh, to hell with Jackson."

Will, in an almost mindless and endless circuit of the house, accompanied at heel by Anvil, tail dragging, brow furrowed, ears and jowls having assumed a despondent and owl-like appearance, confronted at all points by the blackbird. From the edges of roof gutters. From windowsills. From trellises. From boughs and twigs. From cold frames. From piled-up heaps of wood and garden litter. From above in close flight.

From swoops at Anvil. From the ground a pace or two ahead.

"I'm demanding satisfaction, human. You've got to feed a kid regular or you get a sick kid. Especially if you're a bird. First time she's ever been late for breakfast."

Will insisted upon expressing the opposite view. "It's over, dumbkins. Clear off. Go tie yourself to a stone. Go find a high cliff."

"My kid's got rights to her breakfast. You took her away. You bring her back."

Will burst out: "I had rights to my breakfast, too, but what did I get! She was too young to be flying round on her own. You should've taken better care of her. Like you should be taking better care of yourself. Taunting this pussycat. Screeching with a full mouth. You'll choke or get shot down by a claw."

Said the blackbird: "When a bird puts a straight question he's looking for a straight reply. I'm looking for my kid. Until her mother gets here, you deal with me. Know when you're lucky."

"You saw what happened," Will yelled. "Dead is dead. Dead if you're a human. Dead if you're a worm. Dead if you're a blackbird."

"My kid," said the blackbird, "has been brought up on good wholesome food. The very choicest. The very freshest. Hand-reared. Hand-picked. Direct from garden to plate. Try slipping her the rubbish you humans eat and you'll stunt her growth."

Will leant against the house, dazed, while the black-bird paced a windowsill. Tail switching. Beak crammed with worms.

Will pulled himself together with an effort almost out of reason. "My poor feathered friend. You're getting me mixed up with gods and angels. I can't undo what's done. There are standing orders. They're written. There's no way I can start your kid up again. Not for her sake or your sake or my sake. It's not the way things are arranged."

"I'm sick of talk. Bring me my kid."

There was a heap of bluestone gravel bound up with couch grass, and an explosion inside Will.

He dropped on one sore knee and thrust in one sore hand. He'd stood all of Creation he could stand, and pitched handfuls of gravel at bird, at cat, at house, at trees, at rosebushes, at hazards and defences, at Jackson, at the Japanese Second Army, and into the air where the Supreme Powers might have been. And he sobbed from the disappointment and frustration and anguish of coming to the end of something, and set to work on the hazards with rake and fork and spade and axe and stinging hands. Started opening them to the sun. Started gathering them into heaps. Started burning the rubbish, the debris, the rotting timbers. And to the mounting flames committed the broken bottles, the splintered glass, the infested bricks and wood heaps. And said over and over:

"I declare Hadden an open city. No way will I be

defending it or launching attacks from it. The whole thing's a stupid game, a stupid reason for risking my life. Or putting anyone else's life at risk. Standing Order No. 1 will have to work some other way. Getting back up on that ridge to prove a point is for lamebrains.

"It's for lamebrains like birds."

18. Overcoming the Resident Jellyfish

Further concerning the third anniversary of the declaration of war upon Germany by France and Great Britain. And by several distant former colonies of Great Britain.

Eventually, more of Will also in the absence of Mum at Carpenter's of Collins Street. The tearoom at that address and the disappointment of the spring sale. Mum tested severely by general anxiety and clothing coupons and the solitude of her own company.

Plus the usual absence of the Colonel. Up some creek. Keenly and closely supervising the usual urgent survey. Forgetful, as always, of other loyalties and other people.

And of the established absence of Patricia. At St. Augustine's. Being turned into a lady. An activity, according to her teachers, related to quarrying for basalt. A day Patricia in no way recalled, for it was but one of a great many.

And of the obligatory absence of Geoffrey at No. 2 Initial Training School for aircrew. The day Flying Officer Jim Sandal, D.F.C., escapee from Stalag Luft III, recently repatriated from Britain less two legs and the greater part of his life expectancy, lectured the awed school parade on the need to excel.

The first lecture of enduring impact Flying Officer Sandal (1918–1949) delivered during the course of his life.

The first time Flying Officer Sandal was not able to protect himself from himself in public; but the last time that he was unable to conceal it.

But not the first or the last time that he was to leave an Air Force establishment in an ambulance. And not the first or the last time that he was forced to rest, with numerous nurses fluttering at his bedside. One of them, Section Officer Sarah Watts, became his wife in 1944 and began the best five years of her life. And of his.

"James Houghton Sandal is what they call me."

For some moments Flying Officer Sandal considered

his audience and his opening announcement with equal interest, as if aspects of both surprised him, then he said:

"The *Sandal* is for the Sandal family, as those of quicker wit might have determined. The Sandal family makes shirts. As if you didn't know. We've been at it for a hundred and forty years. Tailored-to-measure shirts of distinction. To your very own personal dimensions, no matter how peculiar they may be. If not, then remade, without charge to you. Regretfully, our nearest business address lies six hundred miles hence, so my unprincipled recommendation brings no immediate profit that I foresee.

"The *James Houghton* is a celebration of a great man of the maternal side. A man of much visual impact given to adorning his person with waxed moustaches, usually one at a time, and swinging a walking cane plated with gold dug by his own hand. A man of stern stuff. His portrait in oils, by Asher, hangs above his writing desk in our family home. I, his great-grandson, am twenty-four."

For several moments more he considered twenty-four, then said, "An age of thresholds. Of doors about to open. Of horizons. Of new confidence in the man that one has become. If one can but reach the age and survive it. That much I have arranged, though somewhat torn and worn.

"Which means numerous activities might have been on my agenda for today—had I been left to live my life unmauled by the agents of these madmen who are savaging our beautiful world.

"I could have been abed. Daydreaming. Reflecting at leisure being a divine right of the young man after a lovely night out with the lovely lady. A right I have failed to claim for an unreasonable length of time. Perhaps this morning, in the life put aside, I'd have claimed it as a matter of routine. Rejoicing that the lovely lady might become the constant reality, instead of the daydream.

"Or, perhaps, pressing on regardless with my master's thesis. Greek theatre dominating the dissertation. I have an affinity with the chiton, a garment that would have lent splendour to me, I suggest, in a suitably poor light.

"Or I could have been exerting in the shadow of some closed arena, closed against the eyes of the spies from neighbouring states, striving like the devil to raise the bar an inch or two or three. The national pole-vault title only a short time since having strongly interested me.

"Yet golf might still have been my particular adult enthusiasm out-of-doors. Careful use of the word *enthusiasm* leaving open the sacred place for the lovely young lady. For what greater adult enthusiasm can there be?

"Or might I have been cruising to Fiji? Shirts having sold agreeably well of late. None requiring remaking without charge. Hence a small share moving in the direction of Jim's wallet. Jim making impressions on the way to Fiji, largely among the younger female classes in the vicinity of the swimming pool of that famous ocean liner, now a merchant cruiser bristling with weaponry.

"Or might I be paddling my canoe in some quiet water with the lady reclining under her parasol?

"A thought, my brothers. Which young lady? And where on this day might she be?

"Probably in some wretched uniform drilling on some wretched parade ground, having given her own daydream away. Sadly, not reclining under her white parasol with the lace edges, the gift from me. Looking like there couldn't be anything in the world to gladden more the heart of God.

"In our lost lives, yours and mine, this same September 3 might have fulfilled some special longing, but in the lives we are obliged to accept, how can it possibly be? And for some of my treasured options, as for some of yours, the day will never be. Other options I am striving to regain.

"What are legs but underpinning structures? That they can be removed while one goes on living more or less effectively, suggests that they are disposable, despite one's earnest wish that they were renewable."

Flying Officer Sandal paused to think upon these matters for a short time only.

"Did I start this war? Did you?

"Did I in any way encourage the climate of violence

and vainglory that brought the foul thing into being? Did you?

"Did I rush out to welcome it?

"Shall I grow rich on its profits?

"At its end, shall I live out my life in a welter of self-indulgence? I imagine not. I imagine the same of you.

"But I've had an experience, nevertheless, that I owe entirely to the war. What else do I owe to it? To this new life which has shut down all the old expectations? My presence upon this platform confronting you. Just as you, a body of young men not long out of school, confront me. Without the war, we, as a body, would not exist.

"So the war becomes an experience of companionship in exchange for the life we have put aside, and companionship has never come free.

"So, in the course of this experience I've been forced to face other issues, as you can see. I hope your experience costs less. No one can guarantee that it will.

"In every enterprise there arises the element of chance. Of common or garden good luck or bad. Some people generate good luck like power stations. I remind them that power stations are high priority targets. Lady Luck is found inevitably to be a self-obsessed creature who takes her pleasures without compassion. No person with any brain of any consequence embarks upon any enterprise in the hope that Lady Luck will see him through.

"The enterprise presently aboard is the acquiring of operational background and specific intellectual skills. It's a national duty that you should meet the expectations of your instructors. A personal duty also. You're not in the game to survive, but if you can, with decency, few will condemn you.

"The present enterprise—that continues beyond this place into other schools—is the disciplined study of knowledge that will enable you to complete your operational objectives. You will be expected to strive toward objectives that may appal the spirit within you. On every such occasion, notably the last, it will be your personal objective, come God or the Devil, to complete the mission and return to base honourably alive and well. To come out of it dishonourably alive may not be worth the candle.

"I score the word *learn* in fire on your brain.

"The only safe course you'll ever set on your compass for home is knowledge.

"But first you must absorb a mass of it, and be ready to use it with courage, with a clear head, and imagination, for one day the world under your seat may begin to melt.

"Work at teaching yourself how to think under severe pressure, including raging fright, at every height to which you may climb by design, or accident, or necessity.

"When the cord with Mother Earth is cut, when you're up there unsupported by instructors, when you come to the edge of where you must be if you are to achieve the objectives set for you, an enchanting phenomenon awaits.

"Thought will freeze in you, will seize in you. Your brain will be displaced by the resident jellyfish.

"It will be your immediate responsibility to overpower the jellyfish, to drive it back. And it will be your critical responsibility to upgrade the performance of your body and brain under what can amount to killing pressures.

"Physical pressure. Mental pressure. Emotional pressure. The pressure of gravity, plus or minus. The pressures of severe atmospheric variation. The pressure of blood in your head like a fire hose. And the pressure of that damned jellyfish forever trying to spring the lid of his box to wipe you out.

"Enchanting. He lives within you. And would possess and destroy you, though you may hope to suppress him and impose your will upon him a day or two at a time—upon the strength and substance of what you learn here.

"This is the hour to get into your bones the knowledge and instincts upon which your effectiveness and survival will stand.

"This may leave you with little time for sleep or recreation or entertainment. Try catching up later. If later you can't, tough luck. Living through this struggle is more important than sleeping through it or gratifying other needs.

"You're young and healthy. You can stand the strain. As I stood it. If your foundations are drilled into rock, you can stand it here, and later, when you face the fire. The rock's inside you. In your brain.

"Muscle, my brothers, is out. What's muscle but vanity? It turns to fat. And fat burns in the fire.

"Brain ranks above so-called nerve or dash. What's dash but blind faith and blind hope that luck'll hold out?

"Brain ranks ahead of legs. They can fix you up with bits of wood.

"But foolproof textbooks haven't been written. Remember that. Leave room in the brain for manoeuvre. The textbooks of this war haven't even been written by the aircrews of this war. We haven't had time to write them. So aim on becoming foolproof yourself, because nothing survives that doesn't stand upon itself.

"When the unexpected blows up, the men separate from the boys. The boys panic because they're only boys. They've been too busy mucking about to be anything else.

"The men call upon their hard-learned capacity to recognise, organise, and confront a problem with imagination in less time than it takes an anti-aircraft shell to carve your wing off.

"If you're here in this place you have all the equipment you need to understand what's going on. And then to put it together. The equipment was issued free when you were born. At a cost beyond price. A hundred thousand years or more of human struggle. And you don't start understanding what that struggle was about until evil men start taking bits of it away.

"Get everything put together for yourself. In the hope that you'll be coming through in a single piece, though coming through half-missing, in good spirit, has the edge on coming through dead.

"Put it together for your family's sake. You can't go on with them into a new world if you go for a Burton in this world. The spin of the wheel is always against us, but it's not to say we can't win the struggle and survive. And it's not to say that we'll lose from the grave.

"Put it together for your mother's sake. Even as a girl she bore hurts for you. Give a thought to her giving birth to you. Give a thought to her now; every day still hurting for you."

Flying Officer Sandal, visibly tired, became visibly fatigued, and took a chair from the table at his side and held to the back-rest rail.

"Sit down, sir," someone called.

He remained upon his wooden feet.

"God knows what's going to jump on you from behind the cloud. A cliché of the airman's way of life. Believe me, facing what God knows is no cliché.

"The direct line to God is currently carrying very heavy traffic. Everyone ringing him up. Everyone trying to get through. Everyone wanting His personal reassurance. Even me. Even you. Millions of us urging, demanding, pleading that He should come down and stick the human race together again.

"As I see it, in my better moments, He's already

done for me—and for you—about all in fairness He can be asked to do.

"Some people look for wet-nursing half their lives. Out they go into it, praying Save me, save me. It's awful out here. It isn't fair. I'm only a boy. It's got nothing to do with me except that I got born. It's not fair. It's not fair.

"God helps those who help themselves, my brothers. A simple truth that really does deserve the respect it's earnt.

"Better, I think, to go out saying Help me please, to be the man I'll need to be if I'm to cope with the world that others have made. Help me to meet it with courage and dignity. Help me afterwards to make it new."

Geoffrey, much moved, wrote comprehensively in his diary of Flying Officer James Houghton Sandal, the distant cousin who entered his life by surprise.

In due course Geoffrey's diary went home to the family with only a few excisions. His mother kept the original close to her for forty years.

Will carefully copied the diary in his own hand for his own use and took it with him as an addendum to Standing Order No. 1, and in due course fulfilled his own objectives and Geoffrey's and those of a few others as well. Fulfilling even several of mine, for I wrote his speeches through his great years.

DEAN B. ELLIS LIBRARY
ARKANSAS STATE UNIVERSITY